LAW OF DESIRE

T0125830

Andrej Blatnik

Law of Desire

translated by Tamara M. Soban

DALKEY ARCHIVE PRESS
Champaign / London / Dublin

First edition, 2014

Originally published in Slovenian
as *Zakon želje* by Študentska zal.,
Ljubljana, 2000.

What We Talk About appeared in *The Prague Revue*, 7, 2000.
When Marta's Son Returned appeared in *Edinburgh Review*, 108, 2001.
Electric Guitar appeared in *Descant* 111, WINTER 2000, VOL. 31, NUMBER 4
and *From the Heart of Europe,* Texture Press, 2007.
Too Close Together appeared in *Absinthe*, 1, 2003.
The Day of Independence & *Surface* appeared in
Angels Beneath the Surface: a Selection of Contemporary Slovene Fiction,
North Atlantic Books, 2008.

Library of Congress Cataloging-in-Publication Data:

Blatnik, Andrej.
    [Zakon želje. English]
    Law of desire / Andrej Blatnik ; translated
by Tamara Soban. -- First Edition.

        pages cm

From the short story collection Zakon želje by Andrej Blatnik;
translated from the Slovenian by Tamara Soban.
ISBN 978-1-62897-042-5 (pbk. : alk. paper)
    I. Soban, Tamara. II. Title.

PG1919.12.L38Z3513 2014
891.8'435--dc23
        2014003171

Partially funded by the Illinois Arts Council, a state agency
and The University of Illinois (Urbana-Champaign)
This translation has been financially supported by JAK, the
Slovenian Book Agency

www.dalkeyarchive.com

Cover: design and composition by Mikhail Iliatov
Printed on permanent/durable acid-free paper

CONTENTS

I've been waiting for a guide to come and take me by the hand
Could these sensations make me feel the pleasures of a normal man?

Ian Curtis, *Disorder*

LAW OF DESIRE

What We Talk About

I met her at the American Center. I was returning Carver's *What We Talk About When We Talk About Love*, which I'd been taking longer to read than I should have, so I went uneasily, listlessly, knowing what was in store—the librarian's piercing stare and shaking head when she realized I'd missed the due date by a mile.

To put off facing all that ill will, I resolved to leaf through the newspapers first. It was mid-morning, the reading room was empty—apart from one woman, sitting at one of the desks at the back, reading *Esquire*, with a closed book lying in front of her on the desk. I checked the title from force of bad habit: *Female Criticism*.

She glanced up at me, and I was given a reason for my uneasiness: I had been caught out, an observer, a peeper, a voyeur. I had to justify my look, I had to say something. I didn't have that many options. I asked her if she was interested in female literature. She said that was the only kind of literature she was interested in.

Talking about literature is one of the few things at which I excel. I jumped at the opportunity. I said I wasn't all that sure there was such a thing as female literature. She gave me a stern look. I spread my arms, like: You know what I mean? She said she'd known straight away I was just another typical phallocratic reader.

I couldn't help myself, her directness sent blood rushing to my head. I swallowed and said I'd translated two books by Anaïs Nin. She nodded and said that she'd read them. But she'd also read a third book I'd translated, and that was a typical conservative patriarchal yarn. The man takes care of his family, makes money and all the decisions, while the woman faithfully stands by him and does nothing else. That kind of thing. Typical.

I didn't dare ask if she'd also read the books I had written. I didn't dare ask how she knew who I was. I mumbled something about how I was translating Sylvia Plath's novel at the moment, which actually made me an aficionado of female literature. Unlike her, who read men's magazines. She ignored the jibe and asked me if I really thought female literature inevitably portrays women as helpless, pathetic featherbrains, which was the case, if I was honest about it, with *The Bell Jar*. It was an interpretation that could have been contested, but I reckoned I wasn't feeling up to it.

We may have been too loud, the librarian started to make meaningful throat-clearing noises. Although we were the only two people there—apart from the librarian, of course—this was nevertheless the reading room. I went out on a limb and asked her if she was so uncompromising about the macho act that she'd think me a pig if I asked her out for coffee. She said she wouldn't, she said she loved drinking coffee tremendously (yes, that's the word she used). But that she'd pay for it herself. I said I thought that was fair enough. She got to her feet and slipped the book back into its space on the shelf. For a brief moment I wondered if she hadn't placed it on her desk just to provoke me.

In any case, I in turn tossed my overdue book on the counter with a show of determination, muttered my name, and when the librarian speared me with that look and took a deep breath in order to give me the usual dose of reproof-cum-indignation, I drummed my fingers on the counter top and said we'd chat some other day because today I was in a tremendous hurry (yes, exactly that!). I winked at my new companion, and she winked back.

One thing I have to admit: if there's something physical I'm attracted to in women, it's large eyes. She had them, and on top of that a hairstyle like Glenda Jackson in *Women in Love*. We went across the street, to the Café Tivoli, which everybody still calls Petriček, though the name hasn't been changed for political reasons, and when I accidentally put sugar in my coffee, which I normally never do, I said to myself: Boy, oh, boy. You could have kept that book at home for another day or two. You could refrain from looking at what other people are reading. And you could have avoided speaking to her. Or, even, after all that, not invited her for coffee. Yes, you could have done all those things.

I asked her what she did for a living. (It's hard to talk to a stranger without asking them that sooner or later.) I wasn't trying to follow the advice of more experienced men who say that female intellectuals should generally be avoided, in a way I was just hoping that she'd placed that book there to catch me. Then I might know better whether my female acquaintances were justified when they complained about finding themselves prey. To be quite honest, I kind of desired that role for myself. They do say, after all, that the only thing to be gained in life is experience.

But on the other hand, what should I talk about with her if it turned out that the book was only there as a lure? (Which was a sort of secondary topic to one I was treating in a story I was writing at the time, viz. what can one talk about?) I have to admit, I rarely have dealings with the real world or whatever it's called. Most of the people I come into contact with are like me. We go to the movies. We read books. We listen to music. No harm in that, but it's not real either, so to speak.

And yet: If I've gained anything from all the books I've read, it's rhetoric. The gift of the gab. The ability to answer any question, as long as I feel like it. Perhaps not answer it in such a manner that I'm understood, but definitely so that it sounds interesting.

She said that she didn't actually know what she did exactly. (I would have answered the same, I thought to myself, while feeling a strange sense of pleasure.) She goes to the movies, she reads books, she listens to music. Good, I thought. We seem to speak the same language. I asked her about a film that was enthusing the people of Ljubljana at that time, and she said it was awful. I thought to myself: Here's a girl I could go to the pictures with. Then she asked me which magazines I'd come to read at the Center. I told her none, that I'd only come to return a book. She asked which one. I told her. She said she'd read it and the only part she liked was the title.

This made me almost dejected. I asked why. She said it was too sad, that all the characters talked past one another. I said something foolish, I said: But that's what life is like!

"Right," she said. "That's why."

We were silent. I toyed with the spoon in my empty coffee cup. Well, it's finally happened, I'm at a loss for words, I thought. And on the one occasion when I need something to say. Indeed: What can we talk about?

Although we'd run out of things to say, neither of us claimed to be in a hurry. We just waited and maintained our silence. She looked out the window, I glanced around the café. A young couple were sitting at the next table. The woman was crumpling her paper napkin while he was reading a comic.

"Hon," I heard her say, "why don't you ever talk to me? How come you're always silent?"

"Shut it, babe," he mumbled.

"Sometimes I think you don't love me at all," she continued. "Because you're always silent."

"I love you," he grumbled. "Now shut up."

I peered over his shoulder at his reading matter, and saw a hulk jumping up and down on a tiny fellow sprawled on the ground. The frame had SPLAT . . . SPLAT . . . inscribed over it.

I looked back at my companion. She was looking at me with raised eyebrows. She didn't say anything. We nursed out coffee cups. A waitress came by.

"Can I have the check, please?" I said and reached in my pocket. She did the same. "I'll get it," I said, as I usually do.

"No," she said, "no. That's not fair."

The waitress looked at us in surprise.

"It makes no difference," I said. "Just leave it, it doesn't matter."

"No," she said, "no. It does. We had a deal."

"Okay," I said, "then you pay. What difference does it make?"

"Your coffee too?" she said.

I felt like saying: No, I'll pay for my coffee myself. But I really thought it didn't matter. And besides, the waitress was already looking around. I hate to stall the natural rhythm of the world.

"Yes, if you like," I said. "I don't mind."

She nodded, looking at me. She extended her hand with the money, still looking at me. As I said – large eyes.

"It's okay," she said to the waitress, who was on the point of counting back the change. The waitress mumbled something and shoved the money into her pocket. She moved away from our table, walking backwards, looking at us, until she bumped against a newly arrived customer.

We held each other's eye. I heard laughter somewhere behind me and I jerked my head around. No, it wasn't meant for me. A group of high-school kids were looking at pictures in a magazine they'd just unwrapped from its foil. I knew the magazine. An ex-neighbor of mine was the editor. It was pornographic.

So, it crossed my mind as I was slowly turning my head back, now she's going to laugh at me. And I'll deserve it. For being paranoid.

She didn't laugh. She kept looking at me, right in the eye, and then she nodded.

"What?" I asked, with an edge of provocation.

"Nothing," she said.

For a moment I paused. "Well, then, let's go," I said in a reconciliatory tone. "What are you doing now?"

She shrugged. "Going home," she said.

A good little girl after all, I thought, and admonished myself immediately. Behave yourself, no sarcasm.

"And where's that?"

She told me the name of the street. I'd never heard of it.

"Do you want a ride?"

"Is it on your way?"

"I don't know where it is," I owned up.

She smiled.

"I can take a bus."

"No," I said, "I like driving. And one should get to know new places."

That wasn't very funny. You can do better than that, I again upbraided myself.

She was merciful and pretended she hadn't heard.

"Would you really give me a ride?" she said.

"Why, do you think I was just kidding you?" I said.

"You could've changed your mind now that you've see me in broad daylight."

I wasn't certain she was joking.

"I saw you before. When we crossed the street."

"That doesn't count," she said. "We were talking about books, and when you talk about books everything seems different. More beautiful, I guess."

I didn't know whether she was teasing me or speaking in earnest. It sounded serious, but I knew I would panic and leave her alone if I decided that she was in earnest. So I preferred to think she was just teasing me.

We reached the car.

"Here you are," I said. To hell with 'we'. It entailed more intimacy than I was willing or able to deal with at that moment. I unlocked the door on her side.

Once we were inside the car, with the engine running, I asked: "Where to now?"

"Aren't you going to take me home?" she answered.

"Sure," I said, somewhat puzzled. "But where is that?"

"Just drive. I'll tell you as we go."

I drove nervously, changing lanes, slamming on the brakes. Naturally, I tried to appear as relaxed as possible. And she spoke as though I were taking a driving test: "Over there. Turn left there. Now make a right turn." And then: "Stop there. Here we are."

"Here?" I said. It was the extensive parking lot of a housing development. We were surrounded by a forest of tall apartment buildings.

"I live here," she motioned indeterminately upward, "I can't help it. So, do you want to come up for a coffee?"

"Coffee?" I repeated like an idiot. "But we've had one already, haven't we?"

"So you don't," she said. "Well, then, thanks for the ride."

I felt that she was taking all the initiative away from me, and I couldn't have that.

"They say that going for a coffee is just a phrase, with something else hidden behind it," I said hurriedly.

"What?" she asked and looked at me attentively.

"Well, anything. Having a drink or something. Hanging out together. That's what it's all about. Company."

She kept looking at me.

"For a coffee," she repeated with insistence. "There's nothing behind it. Just coffee. Do you want to come up or not?"

It didn't sound impatient.

I knew if I declined, morally I'd walk away the top dog. I'd have an advantage. But then I would also have to hang out day after day at the American Center if I wanted this thing to continue. And I didn't have the time. But I did have enough to want the whole thing to continue. So I said I would come up.

In her apartment, I felt unusually at home for a place I'd never been before. After a while I became aware of the reason for this sense of harmony with my surroundings: The place was a mess. I have never been allowed disorder, despite it being, for me, the only natural state of affairs. First it was my mother who prevented it. Then the woman I live with. Their rule of thumb is: To put the world in order, one must start with the surface. That may well be true, but if everything is neat and tidy I simply don't feel well. I have somehow never belonged in orderliness.

Here, everything was different.

There were books strewn all over the floor, magazines, clothes. Bras. My woman doesn't wear one.

I tried to conceal that I was glancing around. But she noticed. Of course she noticed. She pretended it was nothing. That it was all right. Guts, I thought. In the bourgeois world it takes guts to invite a stranger into such a mess. Or insanity.

"Coffee, then," she said, not veiling the irony.

"Sure, coffee," I answered. "What else? That's what I'm here for."

"Come on, tell me," I said as the water boiled in the pot, "what do you really do?"

"I talk on the phone," she said. "I talk on the phone a lot."

"Is that so?" I said. "Then we can call each other up some time."

She looked at me seriously.

"I'm busy a lot."

"Me too," I added hurriedly.

"I mean, my phone."

"I don't hear it ringing."

"Today's my day off."

I didn't know what to make of that. Obviously she liked to express herself in an obscure fashion. I sipped my coffee, looking at her. She looked back at me. Without any uneasiness. We were silent.

"And what are we going to do now?" she said finally.

"Now we're going to kiss," I said.

"Oh no, we're not," she said.

"I didn't think we would," I said.

"Then why did you say it?"

I shrugged.

"You thought you had to. But you didn't."

I made no comment on that. "What do you suggest?" I asked.

"We could talk."

"About what?"

"About kissing, if you like."

"It's too innocent," I said.

"Okay, then about something less innocent."

"About what?" I pretended not to understand.

"About exactly that," she said calmly, unruffled.

"You don't talk about it, you do it," I objected.

"You're behind the times all right," she said.

"So what's in then?" I asked.

"Not to do it, but only to talk about it."

"Why?" I said. "Because of AIDS?"

She smiled. "What AIDS! Are you nuts?"

"Aren't you afraid of AIDS?"

"I have no reason to be," she said. "Why should I be afraid of AIDS?"

"I thought that was also in. Everybody I know is afraid of AIDS."

"That's just what women tell you because they don't want to have sex with you."

I decided to ignore that. The woman was capable of low blows. Good. Very good.

"I have a friend who kicks his wife under the table when they go visit his parents, to make sure she doesn't eat salad from the same bowl as them," I said. "Can you imagine that? He's afraid of catching it from his own father and mother!"

"Isn't it nice that he has more trust in his wife than his parents?" she countered.

"Or else he's simply paranoid."

"You like to make fun of other people," she said in a matter-of-fact way.

"Yes, I do," I admitted.

"Me too."

I don't doubt that for a second, I thought. But I didn't say anything. Perhaps I was afraid that she'd say something back. I didn't want to take it any further.

"Aren't we going to talk?" she asked.

"About that? I'm not sure I have all that much to say about it."

I realized that I was beginning to become defensive.

She twirled her coffee cup.

"Never mind then," she said.

Now I didn't know what to say. I gulped down the rest of my coffee. It wasn't good. Too sweet. She didn't ask me how I took my coffee, I thought. She just made it the way she always does.

"Thanks for the coffee," I said.

"Are you leaving?" she asked.

I nodded. I've done my bit, I said to myself. Now I won't have to look around the American Center to see if she's reading some strange book again. An interesting woman, no doubt, but after all, I've got one just like that waiting for me at home. And that one doesn't put sugar in her coffee but drinks it like I do. And of course coffee is in this case a metaphor. It doesn't only mean itself, but everything. Okay, maybe not everything, but certainly a great deal.

I got up. I went toward the door. She followed. If she asks if she'll ever see me again I'm going to say maybe, I thought. Let her hang around the library waiting for me to show up.

She didn't ask. I halted in the hall, looking at telephone cords snaking from the wall into all the rooms. A Babel of cords. I understand she talks on the phone a lot, I thought, but hasn't she ever heard of cordless phones? So you do sometimes get somebody else's line, but at least you don't need to have a phone in every single room. She obviously did. And one in the hall as well. In the little square under the dial there was a number. Simple, straightforward, elegant. I memorized it immediately, without really wanting to. I couldn't help it.

"Bye," she said. "And thanks for keeping me company."

"Bye," I said. "And thanks for the chat."

"I can do better."

"I believe you can," I said. And waited to see what she said. With the 'maybe' ready on the tip of my tongue.

"Okay, then, have a nice time," she said.

I swallowed the 'maybe', nodded, and went out the door. I looked about for the plate with her last name. No plate. Downstairs in the lobby, on the mailbox which went with her apartment (I'd checked the name-plate on her neighbor's door and located her neighbor's mailbox) there were some seven last names. A sublet apartment. Passing from hand to hand. Oh well, I have her phone number and that's more than enough, I thought.

Driving home, I almost ran over a dog that darted across the street, and then didn't notice a traffic light change. I only came to my senses because of the honking of horns behind me. That doesn't happen every day, I said to myself, and made a detailed plan for the afternoon: First up the hill to Šmarna gora with my mountain bike, then a cold shower and to the pictures with my bed-and-board partner; afterwards I'll cook her my Bengali curry and then let happen what will.

Shit. At home I was met by a note: "Brane called and we went to the mountains. I'll be back on Saturday. Good typing. Love."

Of all the days on which to announce prancing around the crests and ridges, she had to choose the very one on which we could have had such a good time together, I thought. But I had to admit that I would have thought the same about any other day as well.

Naturally, I altered my plans a bit. I slapped together some spaghetti, wolfed it down without enjoyment, and then got down to typing. Typing none other than the stupid story about what one can talk about. Understandably enough, what kept occurring to me now was that we not only can, but also must, talk about everything, even about things we used to only do, and talked about only sparingly or, if possible, not at all. But by following that line of thinking I upset the entire structure of little hints I'd been dropping laboriously throughout the text, and the whole thing was now leading nowhere.

I realized I would have to rehash all this stuff about talking, so I called Brane's woman, who, like me, hated going to the mountains. I was going to invite her for some Bengali curry—it's never too late for a curry—and for some serious conversation about talking; and, last but not least, I had to admit to myself, to bring about a kind of symmetry which would enable me, when my partner returned, and with a glint in her eye informed me of the beauties of nature at an altitude of a couple of kilometers, to counter it with an equally zealous portrayal of the enchantment of long conversations with the woman of her high-altitude travel companion.

The plan fell through: Brane's woman was not at home; like every time he went to the mountains she immediately made the most of it and rushed off to see one of her admirers. I knew she wouldn't be back in a hurry and that I'd have to chat with somebody else. But I also knew that most of my acquaintances would find my problem papery, theoretical, artificially construed. Quite unlike Brane's woman, who was game for anything, always took everything seriously and went all the way. Maybe that's why Brane spent so much time in the mountains.

So of course I ended up dialing the number of my morning companion. There were two ringing tones and then a click and her voice, softer than in reality and a tad hoarse: "This is my answering machine. Today's my day off."

I was a bit put out. Her day off, sure. That was the third time I'd heard this today. People are usually at home on their days off, and they leave messages like this, if they leave them at all, on their answering machines at work.

Instead of a chat I called up my brother to see if he had any interesting new films on video. He rattled off a list so long I gave up halfway and settled on Altman's *Short Cuts*. My brother dropped off the tape on his way to the late show at the art house cinema, and as a token of my appreciation I offered him some of my curry. He was so enthusiastic about the idea that I had a very hard time fending off his disappointment when I remembered that I hadn't even cooked the curry and all I could offer him was some cold leftover spaghetti.

My mood finally improved with the film: It was hilarious to watch the young woman feed her baby, change its diapers, and at the same time moan obscenities into the phone wedged under her chin, obscenities for which somebody was paying her money earned from the sweat of his brow. In the meantime her husband paces the apartment, slightly confused, looking inside the refrigerator every few moments. What can you do? Business is business. And then he asks her: How come you never talk to me like this? It killed me.

When the flick was over I surfed the satellite channels for a while until I came upon a group of amply denuded young women who were obviously adding a touch of color to some home shopping network or other, and I stopped there a while. Then I dozed off.

The first thing that entered my mind in the morning was the fact that today I was still on my own, while on the morrow my sweet partner would descend back into the valley. There was no time to lose. If my writing was at a dead end, I had best use the time for social contacts. I decided to give the simple, straightforward, elegant phone number another try and ask its owner how she'd been and if her day off was over and she was back home. I had some tickets to a film preview. That might not be too bad a start to an evening out.

This time there was no click of the answering machine; what came on immediately was her voice, again all soft, yielding and sweet. "Here I am," she said. "Tell me the code."

"What code?" I asked like an idiot.

"Well, the reference code under which you paid the money," she said, somewhat taken aback.

I understood less and less.

"I didn't pay any money."

She was silent for a while, and then she said: "Then we won't talk." And she hung up.

I didn't know what to feel—confusion or outrage. But either way, her expecting I would pay for talking to her set me thinking, and I sat back down to my story and finished it off with the sense that we can indeed talk about everything, but that the only conversations of any value are those which we manage to have after great struggle. I hinted that these would be conversations about things people would absolutely refuse to talk about, for love or money.

I spent the entire day writing the story, I only took time off to quickly broil the chicken I'd been saving for my curry, and every time I got hungry I went and sliced off a chunk. All I had time left for was a shave before I rushed off to the cinema.

I realized I had two tickets, not one, when I proffered them at the entrance, and got a strange look. I drew back my hand and looked around. It was sold out, there'd surely be someone short of a ticket.

Sure there was. And, naturally, it was her. You know the story. You know how these things work. I motioned to her. She approached. What else could she do?

"Are you going to the movie?" I asked. Perspicacious, obviously.

"I'm not."

"What are you doing here, then?"

"I was going to go, but they've sold out."

"Uh-huh," I said. "Follow me."

Blessed miracle-working directness. Nothing comes of the lines: Would you, and if you would, when would you, or would you rather. . . We sat in the back row of a chock-full theater, on the screen a story evolved with a script full of holes, the actors wanted to appear straight-cool-and-fancy and all they managed was sluggish, and we exchanged glances every now and then, smiling, as if to say: The things you have to put up with if you like going to the movies!

The good side of such torture is that it comes to a certain end in some two hours or so; when the lights finally came back on, all of us who'd remained in the theater rose with alacrity, shaking our heads: What shit!

"What do I owe you for the ticket?" she said.

"There's no way I'm going to charge you for dragging you into this misery," I said. "You would've been better off without me, you could've gone for a drink, and not to this mess . . ."

She took the hint.

"If you don't want to take money let's go have a drink," she said.

I jumped at the offer. "Sure, I'd love that."

She glanced around. "Where?"

I took her to a bar where I'd spent my student years. Lately it's become a meeting place for self-proclaimed successful businessmen and is always full, but I know the owner, who has a soft spot for artists, as she used to be something of the sort herself, and when she saw me pleading with the bouncer at the door that there must surely be a tiny little spot left for us someplace (with the thought gnawing at me that my companion would surely be unimpressed by the humility of my approach) she came up to the door herself and took us to a nice little booth. Restoring my position, she even strengthened it by saying that they were saving that table for the President but that he was apparently not coming today, and if he did, they'd figure out something. When I smiled at her gratefully, she just touched my arm and rushed off.

Those large eyes were looking at me, and were opened even wider than usual.

"I've never gotten in before," she admitted. "Okay, yes, during the day, it's possible by day, but never at night."

"Never?" I acted surprised. I shook my head and waved for a waiter.

She paid for the first round of drinks, so I insisted on paying for the second. Then it was her turn again, since I'd given her the ticket, after all, but on the other hand, male pride has its place, and it's just not right for women to pay, at least not to pay more than men. And thus, slowly, having repeated the ceremony of ordering and then arguing about who would pay (the waiters in that bar drank as assiduously as the customers, so the boss insisted on each round being paid for separately, otherwise the numbers got all mixed up and lost) we thoroughly exchanged our views on the development or rather decline of motion pictures since *Casablanca*, touched upon the exorbitance of rents, lauded the new municipal decrees allowing much longer opening hours for bars than in our student years, and so on. Small talk.

From the corner of my eye I noticed that the waiters were placing chairs upside down on the tables the customers had vacated, and I realized the evening wasn't going to last forever.

"Can I ask you something personal?" I said and took hold of her hand. She flinched slightly, but did not pull her hand away. Good. Good. If she hadn't flinched she could have entirely failed to notice what I was doing—we'd drunk enough for that.

"Go ahead," she said.

"What do you do?"

She got confused.

"Do you work on a phone sex line?" I asked directly.

She looked at me in horror.

"No, for God's sake," she said very softly, under her breath. "What makes you say that?"

"I called you today," I told her.

"But you don't have my number," she objected.

"I do."

"Where did you get it?"

"It's written on your phone. Didn't you notice? And as I was passing . . ."

"You called me?" she asked incredulously.

"Yes, I did, and you told me to tell you the code."

She clasped her glass in both hands and tipped back the rest of her drink.

"The reference code under which I'd paid some money."

She became totally engrossed in the marks our various drinks had left on the tablecloth.

I waited a bit, for dramatic suspense to build.

"I asked you a question, if I remember correctly," I murmured confidently.

"Yes," she said. "Yes."

"Don't you know?" I feigned surprise.

She flinched. "What?"

"Don't you know what you do?"

Again she froze.

"It's the second time I'm asking you this. No, not the second, the third time. First while we were having a coffee in Petriček. Then while we were having a coffee at your place. And we also had some coffee tonight, among other things, and I've asked you again. I can't keep up with it at this rate. That's a lot of coffee I've drunk."

"Me too," she murmured.

"Nice, that's nice," I was ironic. "But what do you do apart from drinking coffee?"

"Why do you want to know?"

"Because I have a hunch it's something unusual. The number of phones you have at home—you could be selling them, but you're probably not selling phones—that code thing and all that . . . Have you seen *Short Cuts*?"

"Oh, the one based on that boring Carver?"

My mind fairly spun with indignation, but, to keep the conversation going, I suppressed it.

"Yes, that one. Well, there's this girl in it who makes money by talking dirty to . . ."

She cut me short. "You don't have to spell it out. I saw it, sure I saw it, so what?"

"Well, do you do something similar to that?"

"Absolutely not," she protested hotly. "How could you even think of something like that?!"

"Well, the whole set-up, all those phones you have, the answering machine, the day off when you're not at home, and the way you started talking about the code for money . . ."

"Do I look like that? Like I would do something like that?" she interrupted.

"No, not at all. But maybe that's best for the business."

She looked at me with those large eyes of hers, trying to find the right words. Now I was really intrigued. If I could just make her tell me what people want her to tell them, I could perhaps use it in my story.

"We're closing, sir," muttered the red-nosed waiter and put a chair upside-down on our table. "And ma'am."

She leaped to her feet.

"Yes," she said quickly. "Yes, we're leaving."

The waiter looked at her in surprise.

"There's no rush, no need to panic," he purred leisurely. "There's still the minor matter of paying for the last round."

I threw an approximate amount of money on the table and the waiter scooped it up and stuffed it in his pocket with lassitude. She completely forgot to protest.

When we were out the door she looked at her watch and exclaimed, "What, look at the time! Who would've thought anywhere stays open that long!"

"Oh, there are places that are open even longer . . ." I insinuated. She ignored it.

"There're no more buses," she stated the obvious.

I spread my arms in helplessness.

"How am I going to get home now?"

"You can stay over at my place," I said casually, smoothing out my coat.

She pretended not to hear.

"I live just down the block a bit," I persisted. "A couple of minutes."

She fixed me with her eyes.

"Is your car there?"

"It is," I said, surprised.

"Can you give me a ride home?"

I shook my head. "When I drink I don't drive, sorry. On prin-
ciple," I explained.

She stared at me. "You're kidding me."

"No, it's true. That's my rule."

"This is not the right time for rules," she said coldly.

I could see we were walking on dangerous ground. I tried to
check the pace of the game.

"Oh, all right. I'll give you a ride home. I was just trying a little
harder to convince you to spend the night at my place."

"Why?" she asked.

I couldn't believe my ears.

"I get bored at night," I said coyly. "During the day I count
the neighbor's sheep jumping over a fence, but at night visibility's
low . . ."

"What are you prattling on about? What sheep?" she cut me
short.

I sighed. "Oh, forget it. Let's just get the car if you're going
home. And on the way you can tell me something about yourself."

"Like what?" she said, perturbed.

"Well, like, what you do. Those codes and all that."

"Oh, that."

I was beginning to lose patience. "Oh that, yes. Is it some kind
of secret? If it is, don't worry, I can keep a secret, you can trust me,
I'll keep it safe."

"My story's simple," she said.

I'm glad, I thought. God knows the beginning sounds pathetic
enough.

We'd come to the car. I unlocked the door and started fiddling
with one of those metal bars that lock the steering-wheel. I always
leave the car parked in the street overnight, and I'm told such little
ornaments come in handy.

"Well . . ." she said and fell silent.

I waited a little bit and then straightened up and said: "Go right
ahead, I won't interrupt you."

She was looking past me, and when I turned around I saw three figures taking shape out of the darkness.

"Whatcha doin' here, baby?" one of them said, and the other two cackled. "Come on over here for a squeeze."

I took a good look at them, as good as I could in the dark. I didn't know them, they weren't from my district, and none of them were the guys I gave money to for a drink. They were all dressed in dark shades, just the metal caps on the toes of their shoes glinted.

She stepped back a pace. "I'll just stay where I am," she said.

"Will ya look at that! We got like a little problem to sort out here!" one of them muttered, and the other two laughed again.

"Well, no problem, we'll sort it out."

All three moved in on her. They weren't interested in me at all.

I was aware I had to do something, but I don't have much experience with this type of situation. Well, I knew what they did in the movies, at least.

I took hold of the steering-wheel lock bar and took a step forward.

What the fuck am I doing? I was immediately horrified. But there was no turning back—all three had noticed me. And so had she.

"Take it easy, guys," I said, in a not exactly convincing manner. The bar did not feel very familiar in my hand.

They didn't even deign to turn around and face me.

"Fuck off, southerner," the tallest threw at me over his shoulder.

I suddenly saw red. Who are you calling southerner? rang through my head.

"Come on, guys," I said. "Don't talk to me like that. Or you're gonna get hurt."

That earned me a sincere burst of laughter.

I weighed the bar in my hand, realizing with a certain amount of surprise that it was beginning to grow on me.

"Well, who's gonna go first?" I said. "I mean, that's the way we're gonna play it, right? One on one? Or do you have to stick together to amount to something?"

The tallest one jumped a step ahead.

"Lemme do it, lemme!" he begged his buddies impatiently, and reluctantly they nodded.

"Okay, I guess," one of them murmured with envy. The awareness that they saw me as easy prey gave me a tremendous desire to lift the bar over my head and swing it. But I waited. Don't attack first, I said to myself. Wait, just wait till he gets close, then strike out.

The tall one was eyeing me eagerly.

"So ya want me to kick your ass, huh?" he said and stretched out his hand. He flicked my chest with his fingers.

"The south," I murmured, as the short story of that title by Jorge Luis Borges came to my mind, in which a guy who can't even hold a knife properly engages in a knife fight just because he wants to die in a dignified manner. What a comforting thought.

"What, you wanna go home to die or what, southern asshole?" said the tall one. "It's too late for that now. Too late."

He struck out. I tried to swing the bar, but I somehow couldn't manage it. It just swayed helplessly above me, twirled in the air, and when it touched ground I realized my perfect strike had simply missed its target. Then the tall one lifted his foot, and I saw my companion cover her mouth with her cupped hands. Then I closed my eyes. With my hands I somehow parried the kick. It wasn't half as bad as I'd expected it would be. I could take it. Also, the sense of humiliation was perfectly acceptable. Things like that can't always happen only to other people.

The tall one took a step backwards and I understood it to mean that I should get up. I wiped my face and felt something wet under my fingers. I hoped it wasn't tears. Blood makes an infinitely better impression on women, I thought.

"What, is that all?" I said deprecatingly. The tall one looked at me, perplexed. Perhaps it wasn't very often that somebody asked for more.

Now I no longer thought of fair play. Hit him, I thought. Just hit him. And I did. By some inexplicable coincidence my hand was still grasping the lock bar, and it came to rest in the tall one's groin.

I looked on in amazement, not really realizing how this had come to pass, while he howled his pain.

I knew it was my turn now and that I wouldn't get away with it as easily as I had the first time round. But it was worth it, I told myself.

"Whatcha waiting for? Kick the shit outta him!" groaned the tall one, still strangely doubled.

"The cops're coming, boss," one of his buddies informed him acidly. And indeed, as we two warriors finally noticed, a squad car was slowly sliding up, shedding intermittent blue light on us.

The one they called boss looked around him, appraising the situation.

"Oh, fuck it," he assessed. "Let's get the hell outta here."

And they were already running.

The car stopped right next to me. I was feeling my face, while she was already dabbing at it with some lacy handkerchief. In the blue light I saw traces of blood on it.

"What was that all about?" someone asked behind the rolled-down window.

"They attacked him," she hastened to answer. "First they wanted to attack me, but he helped me and. . ."

". . . he took a beating," the policeman finished for her. "I know the story." He flashed his light in my face until it hurt my eyes. "Surface scratches. Are you going to file charges?"

"File charges against whom?" I asked. "I don't even know these guys."

The policeman grinned knowingly.

"Džajić. That was Džajić and his gang from down south, we know them. Have for a long time now. File charges if you want. Or don't. Suit yourself. Surface scratches."

He rolled his window back up and drove off.

"Well, I never!" she was upset. "Those guys could kill somebody, and the cops would still ask if you're going to file charges!"

"I got off easily," I protested. "After all, I had actively engaged in a fight. They could've locked me up for that."

She gave me a look of gratitude and then asked with concern, "Does it hurt much?"

"Just a little," I tried my hand at histrionics.

"Where do you live?" she asked. "I have to clean out this wound."

"Oh, very close by, just around the corner," I stressed with satisfaction. "Follow me."

I was filled with apprehension the moment I unlocked the main door and saw that the light was on in the hallway. But there was no turning back. I was right: In front of our apartment door there was my woman, with her backpack still on. Her hand was deep in her pocket; she had probably just reached for her key.

My companion slightly released her hold on the arm by which she was supporting me, although it was not actually necessary.

"Where exactly do you live?" she asked, real softly. There are two doors on our floor, there was a chance yet that things might work out smoothly after all. Although she may well have found it strange that I didn't bid my neighbor good evening, or rather, good morning.

"Excuse me," said my woman, looking at me icily, and continued in her guttural English. "I just arrived from Istanbul by train and I'm looking for a friend of mine, Mr. Križnar, but I don't seem to have the right address. . ."

"But of course," I took it up, "Mr. Križnar lives next door, see? This is number seven, and he's at number nine, next door. . ."

"Oh, thank you so much! I thought I'd be spending the night walking around!" she said and pushed her way past us. "My goodness, what happened to your face?"

"Just a minor quarrel," I said. "Caused by jealousy. Jealousy's a terrible thing."

"Sorry to hear about that. Isn't it a shame! And we're supposed to be civilized beings, aren't we? Anyway, have a pleasant night . . . from now on." And she left.

"There are some strange birds flitting around at night in your part of town," I heard while I was fishing for the keys in my pocket.

"Oh, that was nothing," I murmured, contemplating the kind of compensation I would owe my dearest in the near future.

The door finally yielded and I practically fell in. She looked at me seriously and said: "I'm not going to have sex with you, you know."

"Of course not, I didn't think you would. Why should you? We're adults. Come on in."

She hesitated a bit longer and then entered. I fixed her a drink, very gently harnessed the Cowboy Junkies into the loudspeakers, and sprawled in an armchair. She poked at my cuts with cotton wool saturated with some tinctures, which I found a serious nuisance, but somehow I couldn't summon the energy to defend myself.

"Now tell me," I said later, when my cuts were perhaps already healing and when she realized that we would not have sex even if she changed her mind about it, and was duly pacified, "what in God's name is it that you do?"

She took a deep breath and said: "You'll be disappointed. It's not sexual."

"Thank God for that. It'll make quite a nice change if you do something commonplace, like sell insurance or something. Almost everybody I know has worked on a sex line at one time or another. It's obviously the most lucrative business of the century."

"Yeah, it is. And since the supply is so profuse, people have started missing something else."

"Like what? Talking about everyday stuff? Like happiness, football, politics, the price of tea in China?"

"Don't be cynical. It suits your scratches all right, but . . ."

There you go, I thought. Now that I'm making fun of her precious business they're suddenly scratches. No longer are they dramatic wounds, living proof of the injuries sustained while I was chivalrously defending her chastity, but just some unimportant scratches. Oh, all right then. So be it.

"So it's not about stuff that's quite so ordinary? So it is something special?"

She faltered, and finally made up her mind.

"Not exactly. People simply tell me stories they want to unload."

"What kind of stories?"

She said calmly: "The stories of their lives."

I stared at her. Up to that moment, whenever I'd stared at her like that she'd become engrossed in some non-existing point in space, but this time she just slowly nodded.

"I know what you're thinking. Big, pathetic words. They tell me whatever's been preying on their mind. Things they can't tell anybody else."

"What stories are they?"

"All sorts. Some verge on the banal. They tell me how they cheated on their wives half a century ago. Or on their husbands. How they ratted on a fellow worker who'd screwed up something. How they stole a small sum of money. Similarly unimportant stuff. And some stories I wish I'd never heard."

I understood. Stories like the one I harbor. The one I've never told. Or rather, wish I'd never told. Because my woman, when I told her, didn't think it so special. But I do. Because it's mine. Because it happened to me.

I understood. Though not all of it.

"But why do they tell them to you? Why not to some answering machine? Or, even better, to a tape-recorder on their own desk?"

"Because then the story would remain the same. The way they tell it. And they don't like it that way. The way it is, it weighs down on their chests."

"And if they tell it to you, then what?"

"Then I write it down my way. And when they read it, it's a different story. Somebody else's story. And then it's easier for them to decide whether they were justified in letting it weigh on them. Or whether it might be possible, or even more reasonable, to simply forget it."

Yes, there was a logic to her explanation. A slightly bizarre logic perhaps, but then I increasingly find that all logic is essentially bizarre, although it may not seem so at first.

"How do they get to read it?"

"I write it in a kind of third-person narrative. I don't make anything up, I don't embellish. My style's realist, even hyper-realist. All their self-accusations, justified or exaggerated, and all their cheap self-pity and regrets—I leave all that out. What remains is just the story such as it happened. No interpretation. And when they evaluate such a skeleton, their judgment can easily turn out to be different from the one they'd passed before."

"Yes, but . . . The codes, the money paid in advance . . . that must be terribly complicated. Why don't you set up one of those 900-number lines where they just charge an extra rate by the minute?"

"That's fine, but you get the bill for those calls from the telephone company. And if someone, like the person you live with, makes a complaint about the bill, you get a list of all the numbers called. The whole thing doesn't seem very safe. A money order is more anonymous. And the amount is fixed. They can talk as long as it takes to get the story out. It's better this way. Some like to tell it quickly, it just gushes out before they get a chance to change their minds. Others, on the other hand . . ."

She paused.

"Talk a long time?"

She gazed at me with tired, sad eyes.

"For days on end."

"And what do you do in the meantime?"

She was surprised, even slightly offended. "I listen, naturally. That is what they pay for."

"Even if it takes days?"

"It's an occupational hazard."

I mulled that one over.

"That way they stay absolutely anonymous: I don't know who pays the money. I leave the stories at the classified ads office under the code they've chosen, and there they pick them up. I move house a lot, because some of them want to get together with me afterwards. And I don't want that. I don't want any trouble. The biggest problem is that sometimes somebody chooses a stereotypical code, like 'Confession' or something, and then I have to give them an additional code, to prevent confusion, and they don't like it."

I nodded: "Nice. From a distance. You never find out who does the talking. Your clients probably appreciate that."

"They do. And I need it. If I knew the person, or even so much as saw the person, I couldn't write their story objectively. In an uninvolved way."

I considered explaining the scientific theory of how a measurement itself has an effect on the measured quantity and asking whether she didn't think that, when telling a story, even to a total stranger, people adapt it to such an extent that talking about objectivity was completely out of the question. But I was cut short in my musings by the realization that if things were the way she was saying they were, then I couldn't possibly do what I had been contemplating doing for the last couple of minutes: I could not tell her my story. The one that weighed on my chest.

So, then, I thought, what on earth can we talk about? About everything, okay, but does that have any sense at all now?

"Listen," I said, "do you want another drink?"

She shook her head. "I'll get going. The buses will be running now. You don't have to drive me."

So, I said to myself. This is it.

I was unlocking the door, while she was looking around the room as though she had only just arrived.

"You don't live alone," she said. It was a statement, not a question.

"No," I said, unwilling to volunteer any explanations if it came to questions. If she's interested in who and how, I'll just send her over to Križnar's at number nine, and let them do the explaining, I thought sarcastically.

"Are you going to tell her?"

"Tell her what?"

"About what happened today?"

"Sure I will," I said. "Of course I'll tell her. We tell each other everything."

How nice that sounded. Downright wonderful. Except that I omitted something. I failed to mention that we never ask each other anything. Which would make it a useless effort if I tried to explain to my woman that I and the woman to whom she had ceded her place by going God knows where had only talked. Only? Oh, well, let's stick to the conventional ways of the world. They're complicated enough as they are, I said to myself.

She nodded.

"Well, if you tell her, then you'll know what it was."

I continued looking at her.

"I mean this, tonight," she added.

"I know, I know," I said. "There's something else I don't understand. Why did you end up telling me everything? What you do and all that."

She touched my hand. "You know why."

"No, I don't, I don't know."

"Well, it's my story, just that. The one I need to see objectively. Impartially. That's why."

"But," I said, "but . . ."

She waited.

But, I wanted to say, we know each other to a certain extent. Don't we? You said yourself that in that case the story isn't right, that . . .

However, I was already opening the front door and daylight flooded the hallway. On a bench opposite our entrance sat my woman, leaning against her backpack.

She noticed her too.

"What about your friend, Mr. Križnar?" she asked her. "Didn't you find him?"

My woman slowly rose to her feet, put her backpack on, and approached.

"He's away," she said. "Went on a journey, I guess. There's someone else in his apartment."

She nodded sympathetically. "Sorry to hear that," she said.

She leaned toward me and kissed me on the cheek.

"I'm off," she said. "Why don't you invite this poor woman in for a cup of coffee? She's been out here freezing all night. And since you're home alone . . ." she laughed impishly.

I nodded.

"Would you like to join me for a cup of coffee?" I said to my woman, and felt like a complete idiot.

"I'd love that," she said. "I'm pretty cold, to tell you the truth." Then she turned toward her. "I'd like to see you again sometime, but I probably won't. Have a good time!"

She nodded and slowly walked away.

"Let me tell you about it," I said to my woman. "Let me start with how I went to the American Center . . ."

She shook her head.

"Don't tell me anything. I don't want to know. Like you don't want to know how it was for me in the mountains. But coffee, now, coffee sounds tremendously good."

While the water with no sugar in it boiled in the pot, and my woman neatly took her things out of the backpack and transferred them into the closet or the laundry basket, humming contentedly to herself, I realized I had forgotten the phone number. I couldn't remember a single digit. All I knew was that it was simple, straightforward, elegant. So simple, so straightforward, so elegant, that I hadn't written it down.

I could just see myself, driving to that housing development, pressing the bell with an entirely different name written underneath, having some mustached, paunchy seasonal worker in an undershirt spread his arms when I ask him about the previous tenant (*I got this through a cousin of my wife's*), then again sitting for hours on end at the American Center, lining up drinks in bars, feverishly questioning chance acquaintances at bar counters, in the vague hope that they might know her number, asking whether they'd never felt the desire to tell someone what they were unable to tell anybody, and putting up with their suspicious looks, as if I had done something I was later ashamed of and couldn't tell anyone about, anyone except . . .

Somebody touched my hand.

"I'm glad you have nice memories," said my woman, "but you promised me coffee. And look, the water's all boiled away. I'm afraid you'll have to start over again."

I stared at the red-hot bottom of the coffee pot and nodded.

As I always do when I check into a hotel, I first call home. My son answers breathlessly. "It's you, it's you," he cries eagerly. "Mommy, it's him!" Then he asks: "Is there a TV in your room?"

"There is," I say and glance at the tube over which I've just thrown my overcoat.

"What're you watching?"

"Oh, you know. The usual. *Smurfs, Sesame Street*—" I venture, off the top of my head.

"The same as at home?" I can almost touch the incredulity in his voice.

"The same."

"Oh." Incredulity gives way to disappointment. Then he thinks of something else and says: "Have you met any interesting girls?"

"No, I haven't," I say without thinking, while he continues:

"Do they sleep in your room?"

"No, they don't." I want to go on to say: I told you I haven't met any; I want to say: I only just arrived. As though to apologize—

"Mommy, he said no to both!" the little fellow calls out, away from the phone somewhere.

"I said no to both," I repeat under my breath and leaf through my pocket address book.

"Why did you go there?" he asks.

"Do you really want to know?"

"I don't know," says the little one uncertainly. And after a while, as I remain silent, he adds: "Do you want to talk to Mommy?"

"Yes, please."

I can hear his voice ringing out in the hall: "Mommy, it's for you!" And then: "Mommy, come quick!"

My wife comes to the phone. I can hear her shuffling her feet on the hall tiles. I can hear the floorboards creak as she enters the room. "It's you," she states dryly. I remain silent. What can I say? It's true. I can't deny it. I can't add anything to it. What then?

"So, what's going on?" she asks.

"Nothing," I say and feel like an idiot, like a real moron. I pull my coat off the TV set and feel about for the remote control.

"Nothing? Why did you bother to call then?"

Oooh', I think. You can do better than that. You must be having a bad day. A real stinker, even though I'm out of the way.

I zap through the channels. Everything at once. CNN: minor wars at every step. MTV: pretty boys dancing with pretty girls. Business Channel: flickering figures. Babylon Blue: some sort of glossy bodies. Cartoon Channel: *Smurfs*. I hadn't lied to the little one after all.

"It's the proper thing to do."

"*The proper thing?* There's a whole lot of other things that are proper—"

I'm familiar with that pregnant pause. I know it cold.

"Is everything okay at home?" I ask emptily.

"Much better since you left."

"Thanks," I murmur. I pretend to be offended. It's proper. I think.

"Not at all. Thank *you*. For leaving."

"I'll be back," I say, incapable of coming up with anything better. On the TV screen a broadly smiling family mom is bringing a roast turkey dripping with fat to a table ringed by three sons and a husband.

"Oh, that doesn't worry me," says my wife icily. "You'll go away again."

I'm silent. She's silent as well. "Can you put the little guy on again?" I say.

"He's gone to watch TV and he won't want to come back to the phone. I can give him a message if you want," my wife says, without attempting to restrain the malice.

"Tell him I'm watching *Smurfs*," I say. I can't think of anything else.

"He'll be pleased," says my wife. "To hear you have something in common."

*

"I don't know what to do," says Ema.

We're in one of those cafés that few people ever wander into. Ema is fixing me with her eyes, a look typical of a person who does not need to meet many people, and I can see in her eyes that she's not far from tears. She pulls a cigarette halfway out of the packet on the table, then she pushes it back. She knows I hate to see her smoke. I once gave her a badge that said: Kissing a smoker is like licking an ashtray. She laughed, she knows how to laugh at herself, but she never wore the badge. Perhaps it's lying at the bottom of some drawer she never opens. And ever since, she's always glanced at me with unease when she lights up. We do not see each other very often, so I never tell her not to be uncomfortable. Every time we say good-bye I immediately begin to reproach myself for actually enjoying her feeling of guilt.

Ema always talks with me about her unhappy love affairs. If she cannot tell me in person—which is usually the case—she sends me an e-mail. I know what I'll get when I see *Ema@hotmail.com* in my inbox. Ema is a good friend, I know her well, and I know the news will not be good. She does not resort to theatricals to draw attention to her troubles, as my wife would. No trite statements about life having no sense. No accusations flying this way or that. No locking herself in the bathroom, none of that crap. She recaps the facts of what happened. How she met the guy. What he did first. When he told her he wanted to sleep with her. What he was like in bed. When she realized he was not Mr. Right. How she told him. Or, before it came to that, how he told her. Or how he simply never called again. And she never called him either.

I sometimes have my doubts about her, I sometimes think that she is carrying out some clandestine research, of the kind newspapers are so avid for nowadays, and gleefully transforming her apparently daily failures into a precise statistic. But I always have to admire the will with which she tries again and again; it is particularly estimable seeing as none of her affairs has ever worked out, not once. It either transpires—usually after it's too late and she's in love or something—that the man of her choice is actually happily married or not interested in the opposite sex, or else she notices that she's misjudged the situation completely: She should have actually run away from the man she had run after so hard.

Ema is the original woman from the phrase: For a good time, not for a lifetime. Everybody knows that except her, and she is surprised again and again each time her man suddenly decides on another woman and marries her on the double or gets her pregnant or both. Nobody has ever so much as moved in with Ema, though she lives in a spacious apartment she inherited, whose every square centimeter seems to be saying: Too large. Too large for a single person. Never mind moving in; according to her, most men leave without breakfast.

With the last one she thought it would be different again. And she was wrong again. And sent me her e-mail again. And I gave her my usual dose of comforting chit-chat again. And toward the end I included I was going away on a trip and would perhaps be passing through her town. Naturally she wrote back: Come, call me, we'll get together, have a coffee. And now here I am.

"It's always that way," I say. "You know that by now."

I realize: These words only make the matter worse. *Always*, that's heavy—

Ema looks at me, shaking her head. She's noticed that I've noticed how I've put my foot in it.

"Anything new?" I ask. And immediately become aware: That's no good either, I'm asking about news as though these dead-ends of hers were old, familiar stuff, which actually they are, but I should not let her see that, if I mean well, should I—?

"There's someone calling me," says Ema. "That's new."

"What do you mean?"

The coffee is too weak, I bring the cup to my lips reluctantly, perhaps thinking it impolite to leave a full cup, what do I know?

"Calling. On the phone."

"What's new about that? Everybody calls you, don't they? You tell me they call you—"

"Sure they do," says Ema patiently. "But this one's different. The others say what they want. They tell me, in detail. Soon; too soon even. But this one—he's silent. He doesn't say anything. It's different."

"Who is he?" I ask.

"How should I know?" says Ema. "He never says anything."

I am at a loss for words.

"It's really just like you said," she continues. "At the end of the day it's all a question of love."

"I said that?" I play dumb. "Me? I didn't say anything. What do I know about that? Nothing. Absolutely nothing, I tell you. Nothing about questions. I'm not a question man. Answers, yes. But questions—"

Ema touches the back of my hand with her fingertips. I know the gesture. It means: Be quiet.

"You basically don't like me," she says quite calmly.

I'm indignant.

"What do you mean I don't like you? Why shouldn't I like you? Why would I be having coffee with you otherwise? Why would I be sending you e-mails?"

She looks at me and smiles. She keeps me waiting.

"Because you're lonely," she says.

Lonely? Me? That's ridiculous.

"I have to go to the bathroom," I say.

"I know," she nods.

"How do you know that?" I'm astonished.

"You always have to go. Every time we get together. And we've almost finished our coffee now. We'll be leaving soon, right?"

I try to nod and shake my head all at the same time. Then I shrug and hurry away.

*

There are orange slices in the urinals. I grimace at the sight of them washed by the spurt of urine. A distasteful sight. Disgusting.

When I return, Ema is different. She has calmed down, she's also touched up her makeup or something. She looks much better.

"Ema," I say to her. "Ema, listen to me, I want to tell you something too. I can't always just listen."

"Go on, then, talk."

"Ema—" Suddenly I realize that I did not expect this opportunity. And now I do not know what exactly I want to tell her.

"Ema—I have a problem."

"I know," says Ema.

I did not expect that either.

"What do you know?" I actually want to ask: *What kind of problem?*

"You," says Ema, "You're so—"

I look at her and wait.

"What?" I say.

Ema glances around. She moves her spoon around the cup. It's empty.

"Nothing," she says in a changed voice, "nothing at all. Thanks for listening. Now—it's much better now. Can I write to you again?"

"Sure, do," I say, "sure."

Ema nods and starts to pull her wallet out of her bag. Like always, I tell her not to be silly; like always, she insists she will pay; but in the end, like always, she gives in.

When we come out of the café, we see it has stopped raining

while we've been inside. We hug and kiss in a perfunctory manner. The little green figure lights up on the traffic light and I quickly cross the road. I shove my hands deep into my pockets, feeling the lining. After I've crossed I turn around. Ema is looking at me. Slowly she nods.

*

The films were bad, what is the use of being able to see as many as you like on one ticket if they are all lousy. I should have gone out to dine instead of slinking into that hole exuding the stench of stale body juices.

I sit on the bed, contemplating the door of the closet standing wide open, the empty shelves, the metallic glitter of clothes hangers. An unpleasant sight. Obnoxious. Saying loudly: You should—

The telephone crackles. Not rings—crackles. I look at the black box and wait. Nothing. Then it crackles again.

I pick up the receiver.

"Here I am," I say.

A woman's voice giggles at the other end of the line. "I know that," it says.

"Who are you?" I ask.

"You don't know me."

Let's keep it that way, I think.

"What do you want with me then?"

She giggles again. This girl is having a fun time, I decide.

"What do *you* want?"

I look around me. My suitcase is still unopened. My coat is lying on the floor. I haven't even entered the bathroom yet.

"I want to go to bed," I say.

Another peal of laughter. I begin to take pride in my unintentional witticisms.

"Why don't you come down to the bar instead?"

"What am I supposed to do there? I don't know anybody."

A shout of laughter; this is becoming perfectly idyllic.

"You'll get to know me."

"And what good is that going to do me?"

"You'll see," says the young girl at the other end of the line, all of a sudden quite serious. "You won't regret it."

"Oh, no," I say. "Not again."

"What do you mean—again? Has someone called you already?" I can hear some uncertainty.

The competition appears to be fierce, I think. And I have been spotted. At long last, somewhere, I have been noticed.

"They keep calling all the time," I say mysteriously. "All the time."

The uncertainty gives way to disbelief.

"You're kidding me."

I admit to that and think: What now? I sure could do with a drink, how come I didn't buy anything to bring up with me?

"But I mean business," the young girl says, slowly, like reading it from a cheat sheet. "I'll meet you in the bar."

"Are you sure you'll be allowed in?"

"What do you mean?"

"I mean—are you of age?"

I can sense her wavering between taking the opportunity to flirt or be insulted. "You'll see," she says on the down beat.

I wait. I've located the remote control. I blindly press one of the channels and the mute button simultaneously. A woman's face, in close-up. She seems to be screaming. I cannot tell whether in pleasure or in pain.

"Do you want it or not?" she pipes in again.

"What? Someone of age?"

I can feel her patience ebbing away.

"Me," she says deliberately. "Me. Come to the bar . . . Or else sleep well."

"I'm not coming," I say. "Not today. Some other time, perhaps. But not today."

"Oh, you're one of those," says the young girl. She hisses something nasty in an unknown language and hangs up.

*

The bar is a small, smelly hole in the wall, and I've seen too many of them these last few months to remember any one in particular. And it's quite empty. Apart from the bartender polishing glasses in a bored way—a thing that can nowadays be seen only in some television series—there is just one guest. A man. My young girl is nowhere to be seen. I can't tell whether I am overcome by disappointment or relief. Either way, the feeling is overwhelming. Quite different from up in my room.

The man is in some sort of uniform. The army, the marines, I can't tell, the light is too dim and I don't know much about these things anyway.

I make an effort not to look at him. I'm often the only guest in a bar myself and I know how it feels when someone walks in. I step up to the bar.

"Drink?" the bartender asks me.

"Sure, what else is there here?"

The bartender helplessly shrugs and looks at me questioningly.

"Whiskey. No, not whiskey. Something lighter. A cognac."

"Cognac is lighter than whiskey?" the man at my back asks.

I turn around, I have no alternative.

"Actually I don't have a clue about drinks," I admit contritely. "I only drink what I've seen in the movies. And maybe I watch the wrong kind of films."

The man eyes me appraisingly, his gaze travels to my feet and then up again. Against my will I try to recall what I am wearing: Which shoes? Which socks? Which pants? Have I opened my suitcase and changed or am I still wearing what I wore on the plane and at the cinema? I know: I must not look down at my feet. It would be an admission of not being in control of the situation, a proof of my inadequacy.

The bartender delivers the cognac in its globular glass, which I immediately cradle in my hand and start rocking. A feeling of warmth pervades my hand.

"What about you, what do you do?" I try to take the initiative. "Are you in the army?"

It is his turn to look down at his clothes, then he looks up with no small amount of surprise.

"I'm a steward."

"Oh," I say. "I can't see very well. It's dark. And I don't know much about them. Uniforms, I mean."

He nods and waits, as though for me to come up with a better excuse.

"That must be interesting work," I say, to encourage the conversation, realizing at the same time that he probably hears that every time he tells someone what he does.

"Oh, yeah, right," he says tiredly.

"I mean, travel and all that—"

"Oh, yeah, it's wildly exciting to wake up in the morning and not know which country you're sleeping in." He signals to the bartender, who, with a jaded gesture, pours him another shot of whiskey over the ice already melting in the glass.

I know the feeling, I think.

"You meet a lot of people—"

"Too many."

"—and you must have all sorts of unusual things happen to you—"

"Oh, yeah, right." The man leans toward me and I am enveloped by a mixture of vapors: perfume (Calvin Klein, *One*) and whiskey (Jack Daniels, more than one). I like them separately, but like this—

"I'll tell you one unusual thing," he says and motions for me to come closer.

"Please do," I say cautiously and stay put. But to no avail; he gets up and comes up to me, dragging his chair behind him.

"We're flying once on New Year's Eve, that's a real grind, the hardest. First, you can't go where you want, you have to work, that's enough in itself, and then there's all those passengers, each one with their own idea what a New Year's on a plane should be like."

He pauses and tinkles the ice cubes in his glass. I realize with a certain distaste that this is not the first time he is telling the story, it's just part of his usual barroom routine.

"And then?" I prompt him as I suppose he expects me to.

"Then—" he pauses and lays a hand on my knee. I look at his hand, bedecked with rings studded with some sort of precious stones, then I look at him, surely he must see in my face that I don't want that, I think feverishly—

He doesn't seem to have noticed. He carries on with his story.

"There was this woman on board. I mean, not a knockout or anything. Mid-thirties, I guess, business type, a power suit, the works—"

Now he is practically talking into my ear. The bartender has revived and is vehemently polishing glasses, he appears to be absorbed by them.

"And then?" I say. I begin to feel like I am playing a part in some soap opera.

He leans even closer, the smell of Jack definitely beats the scent of Calvin. I shouldn't have left my room.

"Then? First the woman locked herself into the toilet with one passenger. Then with another. Then with a third one. When she was with the fourth one, the flight attendants asked me to go tell her it's against the regulations. I didn't want to, what's it to me, and besides, it's New Year's Eve, let people have some fun."

His hand on my knee grows heavy.

"When she picked up the fifth one and some woman demanded that the pilot make an emergency landing so she could get off, I made up my mind. I went toward her and I felt as though everybody on the plane was watching. Heck, they probably were. When she saw me looking at her she started unfastening her seat belt, she probably thought I wanted some too. I motioned to her to remain seated, I leaned over and I said: Excuse me, ma'am—and she burst into tears right there and then."

"And then?" I say again.

The man looks at me with surprise and takes his hand away. I glance down; I think I can discern a wet spot on my trouser leg. "Then? I don't know. She cried all the way until we landed, maybe longer. I have no idea. We're the last to leave the plane."

I nod and think: What now?

"I have to go to the bathroom," I say.

The steward looks at me, perplexed.

"Fine by me," he says and downs his whiskey, remaining ice cubes and all.

I turn and make my way toward the toilet. The bartender is making a lot of noise with the glasses, but I still catch the voice of the steward as he mutters: "You don't expect me to come with you, surely?"

I have a hard time undoing my pants and I really have to concentrate to direct the squirt at the big pieces of ice that have been thrown into the urinals here. When I return, the bar is empty. The bartender is turning the chairs onto the tables.

"Your friend's gone," he says over his shoulder.

"Ah," I say. "Isn't life good? My first night in another town, and here I have a friend already—"

The bartender upends a chair onto a table with considerably more force than before and glares at me.

"Pay up and get out," he says barely unclenching his teeth. "You get on my nerves, you and your kind. Why d'you have to pick my bar for your meeting place?"

I want to protest, I want to say I was not meeting anyone. I do not protest, however, I don't say a thing, I throw some money on the counter, I don't wait for change, I creep backward toward the door, I dare not turn my back on him. I feel about for the door handle. I can't find it, it's hard like this, with my back to the door. "Easy. Easy," I murmur. "Have a peaceful evening."

"Easy my ass," says the bartender. "I know you. I know your type."

The chair he is upending onto a table hovers in the air for a dangerously long time. He glowers at me, I frantically grope about behind my back, all I touch is cold glass and when I cannot find the handle I finally give in and turn around. There simply is no door handle, that's why I couldn't find it. I push against the door, just as I must have done when I came in, the door gives way and flies backward. I see the moist print of my palms on the glass.

"I don't want your fucking change, you mud-fucker!" shouts the bartender after me. "Shove it up your ass!"

Coins clatter all over the place while I rush up the stairs. What time is it at home? I wonder. *Smurfs* must be over by now—

*

The telephone rings for a long, long time; I start mentally calculating the time difference again. I could have made a mistake, I could have subtracted instead of added, I think. Things like that happen to me. Then somebody answers.

"Is it you, Daddy?" the little one asks.

"It is," I say.

"Yepee!" he shouts.

What shall I bring him this time, I wonder. Has Lego added something new to their Technic program? I can't go wrong with that. Does he have that robot yet?

"What did you do today?" asks the little guy.

"Nothing. I went for a walk."

He sounds disappointed.

"Don't you have any *work*?"

"I do, I do."

"Mommy says you don't. She says that's why you're always traveling some place."

Aah, Mommy. "Hey, listen—"

"Okay."

"Ask Mommy who built the bird feeder on the balcony."

"You did," purrs the little one contentedly.

"And ask her who made your carnival costume."

"You did," he confirms.

"And then ask her who fixed the tire on your bike the other day, just before I left."

"You did," he concludes triumphantly.

"So?" I say. I feel slightly dizzy, I'll have to tell the kid to hang up, I can't talk any longer.

"You're the best daddy in the world."

Tell that to Mommy if you dare, I think.

"I'm not *the* best, but—"

"I know, I know!" he interrupts.

"You do?"

"You're going to say but I'm the best *for you*, right?"

That's right. That's what I would have said.

"Aren't I?"

"Yes, you are," says the little one.

Now the initiative is mine, now I have to follow up—

"What's new with you?" I say and listen to my son ponder.

"Nothing with me, but Gregor saw *Godzilla* on video—"

"Ugh," I pretend.

"It's not that scary. And—" He stops.

"Yes?"

"Who'd you root for in *Godzilla*? Godzilla or the people?"

"The people," I say. "What about you?"

The little one thinks.

"Also the people," he says. And after a short pause: "But why?"

"Because Godzilla's stronger."

"Uh-huh. Gregor was rooting for Godzilla."

"Someone has to root for Godzilla as well," I say.

"Why?"

"Because otherwise Godzilla would be all alone in the world," I say. I realize it does not sound a very convincing argument.

"But—" The little one stops short.

"But what?"

"Nothing." I can sense he's frightened, looking down at the floor, at his slippers, waiting for the right chance to ask about the TV program again—

"Go on, tell me." He has to be encouraged, I have to let him know he can tell me freely what he thinks, that he's probably right anyway, but that there's nothing wrong with not being right either—

"But Godzilla isn't *good*. It stepped on a lot of people. And killed them."

"Aah," I say. So that's it.

"Aah—what?" says the kid. "Godzilla's not good, that's all."

"Sure it isn't good, but—" I know I'm in trouble. How can I explain the world to him if I start from the point of relativism? How can I make him see he must not pull the cat by its tail, that he must clean up, that he must throw organic refuse in one bag and inorganic in another, if Godzilla can trample people and still be allowed to exist?

"That's just the way Godzilla is. It's made *not* to be good to people. Being good is against its nature."

"*Against its nature?*"

"Sure. Everyone has a nature of their own, didn't you know?" I realize I have strayed off the main topic and I add: "And so does Godzilla."

The little one ignores the added bit, the thing that came first is quite perplexing enough. "What does that mean?"

"It means that something larger than you makes you do the things you do most often."

"Uh-huh," says the little one.

"Do you understand?"

"Sure I do." Slight indignation. "It's my nature to play—"

"Exactly," I say.

"—and Mommy's nature to get mad—"

Exactly, I think.

"—and your nature to travel—"

To run away, I think.

"—and Godzilla's nature to step on people."

"Exactly," I say. "And besides, it did all those things to find a nest for its babies if I remember correctly, didn't it?" I search in my memory uncertainly. Was that the American Godzilla or one of the Japanese ones? Or have I mixed it up with dinosaurs? There are far too many fearsome creatures populating video tapes. What happened to the days when children's heroes were fluffy puppies and similar cute things?

"But—" I hear my son pause, whimper, then start sobbing without restraint into the phone.

"What's the matter?" I say and wonder whether his mother is within earshot.

"But—who took care of the baby Godzilla? The one that came out of the egg at the end of the movie? When they've already killed its daddymommy?"

There's something illogical in this story, I think, I seem to remember something about the asexual reproduction of those creatures, but anyway, what is he trying to tell me—?

"Now it has to be on its own, all alone," my son manages to get out between sobs. "It's all alone. Without daddymommy. And it's hard to be alone, it's dangerous—"

"It'll manage," I say tentatively. "Godzillas always manage—"

The little one draws in his breath and the sobbing stops.

"Daddy," he says gravely.

"Yes?"

"Come home. It's dangerous on your own."

I look about the room. I still haven't opened the suitcase—

"I will," I say. And think. Godzilla? Does Lego make Godzillas too?

"Daddy—come soon."

"I will. I'll be there soon."

"If you come, I'll help you."

"Help me?" I don't understanding what he's saying, I don't understand him too often—"Mommy says you need help. You just tell what I can do to help—"

"Aah. Tell Mommy I'm feeling much better since—"

I falter. Since when? Since I left?

"Daddy?"

"Yes?"

"When are you going to stop going away? Mommy says you can't just up and go all the time."

"I'll stop." Maybe when she starts leaving—

"Daddy?"

"Yes?"

"You'll come back before I die, won't you?"

"Sure I will. Where did that come from? You're not going to die!"

"Godzilla died, even though it was very strong. Stronger than me. Much stronger—"

"It was different with Godzilla."

"Daddy?"

"Yes?"

"It was also stronger than you. Please, Daddy, come home."

*

"You're leaving sooner than you intended," observes the receptionist.

"I don't care for the hotel bar too much," I say.

"So everybody tells me," he mumbles uncomfortably. "But there are other bars in the town."

"And hotels too," I mutter.

The receptionist nods solemnly as though that were the only thing he ever thought about.

"As a matter of fact," I add, "there are other towns as well." Suddenly I feel an unbearable pressure in my lower abdomen and I start glancing around the lobby—

"I forgot something," I say to the receptionist as he eyes me suspiciously.

"Would you like your key back?"

I clutch my groin, become aware of the gesture, take my hand away, and nod.

He nods as well.

"There you are, your room's paid for until noon."

I whisper a word of thanks, mince to the elevator, press my thighs together and stare at the lighted numbers above the door. As always, the key jams at first, then in the bathroom I lean my head on the cold tiles and watch the jet of urine gushing into the toilet bowl. Then I drag myself over to the bed. There's no rush, I tell myself, I haven't bought my ticket yet, I can lie down for a bit. I feel the contours of my body on the mattress.

The hotel room is dreary, the open door of the empty closet gapes at me, I can't close it, there's something wrong with the lock mechanism. The suitcase, I suddenly remember, I left my suitcase downstairs.

I dial Ema's number, listen to the ringing tone, then hear her say softly: "Hello?"—so softly, as if she might wake somebody. I wait for a while and then put down the receiver and picture Ema still holding hers in her hand, thinking about which of her men has called. I can feel her placing it down on the pillow next to her. I listen to her body, her breathing.

"I'd like to be closer," I say under my breath. "Closer."

Too Close Together

out of your shirt, PT

The man sits in the gloom of his hotel room, dipping his fountain pen into a solution in a saucer. He painstakingly adds lines to the stamp on a passport photograph. He thinks about the ink, how it will dry overnight. He worries whether the photo really will be indistinguishable from the original. At least at a precursory glance. Yes, that's what matters. He lifts the photo to the dying light and thinks: That's what matters. Matters enormously. It must look as though nothing has been changed. As though no-one has been anywhere near this photo.

A woman's face in the picture—young, her eyes glitter, even the photographer's inability to take a focused picture cannot hide that. This incompetence angers the man more than necessary. He looks at the picture and wonders about the lines he has added to the stamp: Has he drawn them finely enough? Close enough together? He does not ask himself why he is doing it. As is usual in this kind of story, the face reminds him of another woman, a woman he has long been trying to forget.

There comes a cautious, muffled knock on the door; the man gets up, clears away the passport and the pen, steps to the door and opens it a crack, blocking it with his foot. A woman's face pushes in through the sliver of light coming from the corridor. It is the same face, now all in focus, alive, real. The man takes his foot away, the woman enters. She wraps her arms around him and he puts his hands on her hips, slowly, almost with restraint, in a gesture he still seems unaccustomed to.

"Has anyone seen you?" he asks quietly.

The woman shakes her head.

"Did you do what I told you to do at home?"

Now the woman nods. Her words string along in short, staccato volleys. "I did. Left a note. Not to look for me. That I'd write. That they'd follow."

"No baggage. Don't forget, no baggage."

The woman nods again. "Of course. Of course."

"Starting tomorrow, you'll be somebody else. Starting tomorrow, it'll be taken that you, just like everyone else who comes here, have come to look, go back, and spread the word about it. As quickly as possible. And people like that, don't forget, travel without baggage."

"I'm not stupid," says the woman impatiently.

The man nods. "No, you're not," he says.

His eyes search her face. You're not, I really hope you're not, he thinks.

"You've got a new name," he says. "Here, in your passport. Don't forget it. Better still, forget everything you've known about yourself so far."

"Okay," says the woman. "I'll forget everything. I like that. I like what's new. New is good."

The man nods wearily. He examines his handiwork. It could do with a few finishing touches, he can see that, but it is too late now. Darkness has blotted out what's left of the town, and there will be no electricity. Besides, the whole building shakes with the explosions; his hand could tremble. And with a stamp, if you examine it closely, it's the details that count. The nuances.

It's nighttime. The man lies in bed, staring at the ceiling, imagining the many possible courses events may take, thinking about the body of the woman sleeping by his side. About the days and years to come. He can picture some sort of bungalow, with plenty of framed photographs on the walls, a door opening onto a garden, a lot of washing hanging there to dry. The picture is very vivid, his nostrils even fill with something akin to the smell of home-cooked soup. The kind of coziness usually found only in old family snapshots. He wishes for children's laughter to ring out in the background of the picture, for letters from abroad. And he feels slumber washing over him.

Then his eyes tingle. Light crawls over him, the dawn is breaking and everything is different—other smells, sounds, images. But the woman is still there, asleep, she was not just a dream. It is all true: This woman, this place that seems so unreal, the patter of gunfire in the hills nearby, the skeletons of torched houses all around, their departure that is no longer a night away.

He touches her bare shoulder and she opens her eyes.

"Is your mind made up?" he says.

The woman's eyes betray surprise.

"I made up my mind a long time ago," she says. "Long ago."

"I mean," he amends, "you haven't changed your mind? Because if you have . . . This is your last chance. You know?"

The woman looks at him for a long time. Then she slowly shakes her head.

"I know this is my last chance," she says. "I know that."

As they exit the charred hotel lobby the man looks one more time at the brownish smudge on the sidewalk in front of the entrance. Though he has taken a picture of it over and over, in all kinds of light, it always tells him the same thing. If only I could, he thinks again, photograph the eyes of the man who fired the shot, just once, instead of all these drying puddles of blood, then maybe for once I'd have a different story to tell.

A haze seems to be rising off the pavement. The man hands a folded hundred-dollar bill to the boy who's poured a plastic bottle of gasoline into his car tank. The boy shoves the money into his boot, nods grimly, grips his hand in a handshake and disappears behind a corner. The man looks after him as though he has a question to ask. Then he shrugs and tosses the bags with the cameras onto the back seat.

The way out of town has changed, thinks the man. When he drove in, there weren't so many burned-out cars. And they weren't all facing in the same direction. It's changed. So much has changed. Perhaps too much.

The soldier standing by the barricade has unbuttoned his shirt to the waist. He is smoking. Bending forwards to the car in front of them. The man can hear his voice as he asks to see the papers. A hand stretches out of the window and the soldier looks at the passport from afar, with a grimace barely concealing disgust. The man can see: It's a foreign passport, just like his own. And hers, now.

The soldier gestures. The driver in the car up front carefully negotiates the scattered gasoline drums. The soldier bends over and stuffs the bottoms of his trouser-legs into his boots. Then he glances at the next vehicle.

The woman in the passenger seat, her eyes sunken from months of hunger and fear, still seems as beautiful to the man as the angel of destruction. Just like the first time he laid eyes on her. The passport is in her lap. The man wishes he could pull over and check that smudged stamp one more time. But he does not pull over: He knows it is too late.

His colleague. His girlfriend. His wife. What sounds better? Which one sounds right, so right that the soldier does not need to dial a number and ask if anyone else knows about her? Because if he has to go into explanations, the story has several holes in it. Too many. They could disappear down one of them.

As a matter of fact, thinks the man, I've gone too far. I'm too old, he tells himself. I can't focus very well any more. Things have begun to flow together, the dividing lines are increasingly unclear. It's time to quit. Step down. Cash in the savings. Sell the equipment, sort out the negative and positive prints, put things in order. Yes, leave things in order. Prepare for the final hour; next to an open fireplace, in loose-fitting slippers, poring over a chess problem, with a sleeping cat in his lap.

The soldier motions for him to drive on. The man smiles. He knows you have to smile; that way everything's easier. Beads of sweat trickle down his face.

The woman looks at him through slit eyes.

"I don't like your shirt," she says finally. "It has too many stripes. Too close together. No, I don't like it. When we finally get out of this hellhole you'll get yourself a new one in the first town."

A Thin Red Line

When Hunter arrived in Ayemhir the village was shrouded in twilight. The children had begun to screech the moment they spotted the unknown figure, but when they could make out his white, almost translucent skin, they became embarrassed. They huddled in a group and covered their genitals with their hands. *Mzungu, mzungu,* they whispered to one another. Hunter nodded and waited.

Next came the headman. Hunter handed him the bag of salt and told him the name of the sender. The headman scowled, and Hunter felt that the young man he'd met on one of his drinking tours of the waterfront dives, who'd told him to go visit his village, was less popular with the villagers than he'd bragged he was over his drink. But it was too late now for Hunter to change his mind. The bus only came to these parts once a week, when there was a bus service at all.

The headman addressed him in his guttural tongue, of which Hunter could not comprehend a syllable. The old man repeated his jabber two more times, then gave up and summoned somebody who spoke a little Swahili. Hunter tried to explain in the best Swahili he could muster that he was not really fluent in that language either and then asked for the use of the empty hut, the kind that is available to visitors in every village. The headman nodded and kept nodding, then stared at Hunter for a long time, apparently pondering something. Hunter could feel the rivulets of sweat trickling down his back. It was such a long walk back to town.

Suddenly the headman seized Hunter's worn backpack and weighed it in his hand. Instinctively, Hunter's hand shot out. Ever since the mugging he'd mentally practiced this gesture, every time he was scraping the bottom of his tin plate at some road-side eating stall or entering notes in his travel journal: A passing thief tries to snatch his backpack, but he's quicker, he grabs his bag, maybe even the thief's hand, and everything's clear, it's all resolved. There is no doubt. But the situation had never occurred, all his alertness had proven pointless, no-one else craved his traveler's possessions. And now he'd reacted at the wrong moment.

The headman gave him a questioning look, and Hunter thought he had caused his own undoing. How could they take into their village someone who didn't trust them? Out here in the bush feelings must be mutual, as equally balanced as possible. If he does not trust them, how can they trust him?

He tried to mitigate his mistake, pretending on an impulse to need something urgently, but what could a man who had possibly just been granted a roof over his head—the only thing available in the village—so urgently require? His best option, he decided, was to pretend he wanted to give the headman something else in addition to the salt. He rummaged through his backpack, but after his long months of wandering there wasn't much left. His fingers finally encountered a smooth surface: His little shaving mirror, from the time when he still bothered to shave. He wouldn't be needing it now, he realized. He handed it to the headman.

The headman accepted it cautiously and diffidently looked at his own reflection in the small rectangle. Then, becoming rapt, he began to study his image, bringing the mirror close to his eyes and then looking at himself from a distance. He seemed to find the face in the mirror familiar, but not familiar enough to address.

He did address Hunter, though. Actually, he addressed the mirror, and the man who spoke some Swahili nodded and translated. But Hunter did not understand a word, except for *mzungu*, foreigner. Helplessly he shrugged, and equally helpless, the translator shrugged too. The headman nodded and uttered a single word: "Mary."

The children shrieked and rushed off toward the edge of the village. The translator shook hands with Hunter, squatted before the headman and began to retreat backwards. The headman motioned to Hunter to sit down. Hunter looked at the ground, at the exact spot the headman had indicated, and automatically wiped off the dust. In vain: There was only more dust underneath.

Then they waited in silence, until a woman approached, squatted in front of the headman, and said to Hunter: "Welcome."

Hunter thought he had gone out of his mind. Ever since he had drunk water from the village well in Gamendi he hadn't felt exactly clear-headed, but rather as if his eyesight and hearing might have been affected. In any case, this was the first English he'd heard since he spoke to the two Frenchmen who were driving the stolen car across the Sahara and who had taken his money-belt and his papers. They'd had a simple strategy: A knife blade against the throat. All the boot camp training Cherin had made him attend was of no avail when he came into contact with the sharp, cold metal. He did not feel excessively humiliated, though; after all, he had spent most of his training pondering how he was not the right guy for the job.

"Do you speak English?" he asked. The woman nodded.

"I do. Call me Mary. My real name's different, but I'll be Mary to you."

"How come? Where did you learn English?"

The woman smiled at his astonishment.

"I went to university in the United States. Washington D.C. I never graduated, though. I stayed on for a while and worked in an African restaurant, and then I came back."

"Why did you come back?" Hunter realized the insolence of his question the moment he uttered it. If he'd come to this village, why shouldn't anyone else? And in particular someone who'd departed from here sometime before?

"If you can't change the fate of the majority, you must share it," said the woman and looked at the ground.

The sentence had an oddly familiar ring to Hunter. It sounded vaguely similar to what Cherin might resort to at a cell meeting when he ran out of arguments in favor of suicide missions. Cherin kept sending him the same incessant questions by e-mail: Why did you run away? Why did you desert us? Hunter never answered;

what would it serve to reply to the people he was actually running away from? If he had needed to decide on a single answer, though, it would probably have been: Because of stale rhetoric. That would cut Cherin to the quick.

The headman touched Hunter's hand and began to speak. He spoke for a long time, and the young woman translated it all in a single sentence: "He's glad you have come to our village."

Hunter took a deep breath. Finally the moment had come, the moment he had been musing about ever since he had decided to leave everything behind and travel as far away as possible. He suddenly felt it was of utmost importance how he formulated his question. Then it dawned on him that all his caution was immaterial: He was totally at the mercy of the translator, who could twist his words around any way she chose.

"I've come in search of the Nameless One," he said. And hoped that she would understand him, that she would find the right name in their unearthly language for the Nameless One; that the headman would nod; that he, Hunter, would finally find what he had been seeking.

The woman did her translating. The headman scowled and gave her a piercing look. The woman repeated her patter one more time, and now the headman nodded at every word.

"The Nameless One," he enunciated, in English that sounded no worse than Hunter's. Then he continued in his own language.

"He says it's an honor to meet the Nameless One," explained the woman. "He says it's a great privilege to have the Nameless One in his village."

Hunter felt the temperature rising with every word. The earth, it was not even earth, just pounded dust under his legs, emanated heat in waves.

"Well," he said, "well—" He knew what he wanted to say, he wanted to ask: Who is he? What is the Nameless One like? When is he coming? Can I see him? Can somebody introduce me? A thing like this can and must only happen here, flashed through his mind, only here, in this hole in the back of beyond, where else if not here, where things haven't changed their names hundreds of times, does this village have a name at all, it does, but I can't recall it this minute, nobody knows it, not even on the bus where they looked at me strangely when I shouted for them to stop, to pull over for Christ's sake, and then I walked for a long, long time, I walked until my mouth was all dry and it's still dry, so dry that right now I can't say a word—

The woman waited. To Hunter it seemed as though he could discern scars on her ankles, the kind that leg irons would leave, but he could not be absolutely sure.

The headman said something and the woman translated it immediately.

"You've finally arrived in our village."

Hunter did not understand.

"Were you expecting me?" he asked, surprised that his voice found its way through the stuffy heat, and they both nodded simultaneously.

"Why were you expecting me?"

"We need you," said Mary.

Wrong, thought Hunter, wrong again. Like so many before. Like too many times before. Far too many times for him to believe in coincidence any more.

"If you need money—" he felt about in his pockets, but knew all he had could not be changed: He only had a few fifty-dollar coins left.

The headman shook his head and Mary translated his motion into English without hesitation.

"We don't need money," she said. "You're here to give us something else, something that will be truly helpful."

Resigned, Hunter nodded. Cherin always said we had to get to the point where money wasn't the most important thing in the world, and I've arrived there, Hunter thought sarcastically. He waited to hear what the something was.

"Rain," Mary expounded.

"Rain?" Hunter glanced at the dry ground and then at the dry sky. Both looked equally unreal to him, equally unchangeable, eternal.

"Rain," started Hunter slowly, pondering the right words, "does not depend on me." Nothing depends on me, he reminded himself. But he did not say it.

The headman murmured something.

"The juice of life comes from the belly of creation," translated Mary. It sounded somehow solemn, somehow elevated, as though Cherin was about to give the signal and they would burst into song.

"I don't understand," said Hunter.

"There's only one way out of a drought. Only one solution."

Hunter waited. Mary looked at him and he felt as though he could read in her look more than just the search for the right words to translate. She was sizing him up, weighing him, as though she were picking him out of a brood of similar specimens and fretting about whether she'd made the right choice.

"After a long drought, it is customary for the headman to sacrifice himself in a special ceremony."

"In a special ceremony?"

"He slits his belly and soaks the earth with his juice."

Blood-soaked earth. That's a sight Cherin would thoroughly enjoy, thought Hunter. He should be here now—instead of me, he wished.

"I can see why he's putting it off," he said.

"No, you don't see," said Mary softly. "Not yet."

Hunter looked at her questioningly.

"Our lore has it that sometimes a foreigner comes. Who's got more juice. So that after *his* sacrifice it rains longer."

Hunter's head spun. In his mouth he could feel matter throbbing, he felt his tissues fighting for liquid, and he licked his lips.

"You're making it up," he tried to reason. "You're trying to scare me."

Mary shook her head.

"It's common knowledge. Everyone in the village knows it. That's why they're so happy you came."

"Happy?" Hunter could not see anyone. Just the woman and the headman. The children now kept their distance.

"Happy," she confirmed. "There's going to be plenty of rain."

Wrong. Wrong again, as so often before, thought Hunter.

"I have no intention of slicing open my stomach," he said. He tried hard to smile, but Mary's glare told him he had not quite succeeded.

"You don't have a choice," she said, surprised. "You don't have to share the fate of the majority. Because you can change it. You don't have to die of thirst. Because—"

Because I can die of losing my own juices, thought Hunter.

"Do you believe in this sort of thing? You went to university—"

"Yes, I do. I studied anthropology," said Mary.

Hunter nodded and suddenly felt tired, very tired. It occurred to him that he hadn't checked his e-mail in a long time. That for a long time he hadn't kept up with what was going on in the world. Cherin might have been tracked down and shot dead. Hunter might be the only one of the cell still being searched for. Perhaps they had even stopped looking. The only one who never gave up was Cherin. The others were not so tough. Cherin told them they were bored children, that they were there just for the hell of it. Because they'd thought it would be fun to shoot cops and throw bombs and so they joined the cell. And Cherin told them over and over that the old had to be demolished before the new could be established. And so they demolished. For others, Cherin would say. We're not doing this for ourselves. For others. Everything was for others. Cherin was a believer. And if he was gone—

Mary touched his hand.

"Come with me," she said.

Hunter hesitated. He felt it was all a bizarre misunderstanding, that he only had to find the right word to clear everything up, but he couldn't think of anything, anything at all except the face of the child he could never forget, and the woman's hand, the hand of that woman who was everywhere with him, eternally reaching out to grasp the door handle—

"Where?" he said.

"Not far. You've come to the right place already," said Mary, "and we're almost ready."

Hunter thought of the plane ticket he'd carried around in his shoe ever since the encounter with the Frenchmen; they'd graciously let him keep it and advised him to use it as soon as possible, that he was not cut out for these rough parts. All the time it was in his shoe, he'd told himself that he could not use it, that it was a useless piece of some useless stuff from a useless world he no longer belonged to. And maybe he had been wrong, except now. Because now it would be true forever.

The man who suddenly materialized by the headman's side, holding a brightly colored spear in his hand, nodded at Hunter amicably. Other warriors came closer, and when Hunter did not move, they started jostling around him. Every last one of them patted his shoulder and grinned widely.

"Our man," said one of them in Swahili and they all nodded.

What Cherin wouldn't give to be in my shoes, to bond with the simple folk so easily, thought Hunter and he had to start laughing. The guards were elated by his mirth. They dropped to their knees in front of him and rolled around in the dust. He heard drumbeats accelerating somewhere, and guttural cries syncopating with the rhythm, and approaching.

You're always making up your mind first, and then having second thoughts, Cherin wrote to him. In a tight spot you run off with your tail between your legs. You get lost, like a dog without a master. Like that time in front of the embassy. All you had to do was cross the threshold and the mission would've been accomplished. But you chickened out, you dropped the bag and ran. And then that poor woman who came begging for a visa got blown up. And her child. And the cell got a bad name. Killers of women and children, instead of exterminators of the class enemy. There's a fine line between an unnecessary, pathetic, pitiful death and a world-changing one. And you don't know how to cross that line.

The line, thought Hunter. To draw the line. In some languages this means to set a limit, in others, to escape. Who knows what it means here.

The headman stood in front of him. He drew a knife from his belt and proffered it, holding it by the blade. When the handle settled into Hunter's palm, he realized with sudden clarity that all those men in illegal joints in the port who'd told him that the Nameless One could be found in Ayemhir had not been spinning a yarn; He was here alright, waiting. For Hunter.

The headman spread his arms. Hunter knew there was no other way. He nodded and the headman nodded back at him. Hunter could read contentment in the headman's face, happiness that this sacrificial man from the far-away white world, who was about to save the desert from drought, had come to his village and no other.

Hunter took the knife, poised it against his abdomen, leaned on it and cut. At first he could only see a thin red line. On his cheeks he felt the first drops of rain.

When Marta's Son Returned

When Marta's son returned from the war it was evening. He did not say anything, he just kissed his mother on the cheek, flung his duffel bag on the couch and went to the fridge. First he downed a whole can of beer in one gulp, completely ignoring the cookies Marta had baked for him, then took a shower, shaved, and put on his jeans and a T-shirt. He rolled his fatigues up into a ball and stuffed them into the trash can. Then he sat down on the couch and watched television.

He watched television for about three weeks, and his mother, who brought him food and drink at regular intervals and made sure there was always plenty of beer in the fridge, became apprehensive. One day she asked him: "What are you going to do with your life? I've saved up some money. If you'd like, you could try to take up something new . . ." Her son looked at her and shook his head, and it occurred to Marta for the first time that her boy was more than just beat, or even burned out, as she had thought until then.

He said calmly: "I've tried everything, Ma. Everything."

Marta waited. She felt that her boy was on the verge of opening up to her about the terrible things he had been through, the hunger, the cold, the exertions, the friends who had never returned from combat, the blood perhaps, the eyes wide with fear. But her son remained silent. He remained silent, looking at her until tears welled up in her eyes and she ran into the bathroom. When she came back, her son was sitting in front of the television set, the same as always.

Her hope that things would sort themselves out faded. As Marta pondered what she could do, she recalled that her son used to write to Santa Claus—asking for the same present year after year, a present she could never afford, an electric guitar. And she thought that an electric guitar might help, seeing as everything else had failed. She did not have a very clear idea, though, what such a thing actually looked like, so she sought help from her neighbor's son, who was sure to be familiar with technical things, as he spent days on end lying under his car, pulling out different parts. When she finished explaining her request, her neighbor's son just nodded and made a phone call. The pawnshop delivered the guitar to her doorstep; apparently there was a surplus of this type of item, so many guitar players having not returned from the war.

When he saw the black guitar, Marta's son nodded, turned off the television set and took the guitar to his room. And from then on he stayed there, playing the same Hendrix piece, the *Star-Spangled Banner,* over and over. Marta felt that her son was making progress now that he'd taken something up, until one day she realized with dismay that her boy always stopped at the same place, always at the same note. But she bided her time, screwing up her courage and warding off despair, until she managed, during one of his infrequent forays into the kitchen, to ask her son how he felt with that black guitar in his hands.

The boy looked at her as though she was his worst enemy and his hands began to tremble. Marta considered crying out to her neighbors for help, but immediately remembered that, for quite a while now, they always pulled down their blinds the moment she stepped in the front yard; she finally understood why.

"The melody ain't right, Ma," said her boy, as though he found it hard to talk about such unpleasantness. "It pretends to be right at first, but it ain't, not really. You can hear it too, can't you?"

Marta nodded, said she could hear it too and then asked him why, seeing as he practiced so hard, he still kept stopping, hopelessly. Why, despite everything, it just wouldn't work?

"It's the fingers, Ma," said the boy.

"What's wrong with your fingers?" Marta felt a surge of anxiety, an all-pervasive feeling that she had missed something she absolutely should have noticed.

Her son gave her another troubled look and then slowly explained, as though it was a thing that should have been clear to any child: "But Ma, these ain't my fingers."

To substantiate his words he held out his hand and extended his fingers. Marta examined them closely, remembering them as they had been at the very beginning, when they held her breast while his mouth was clamped to her nipple. They still looked the same to her, except that they were to some extent grown-up, although still not entirely. But she did not know how to tell him this, because now her boy seemed so convinced that things were different, something surely had to be.

"I don't know how they got here. Or where the old ones went," added her son while he studied the fingers on his hand.

"But . . ." said Marta, wondering how she could argue with him, since she had no answer to give. She laid her hand on his shoulder, her fingers moving along his T-shirt, and felt his body pulsate underneath the fabric. It flashed through her mind that her boy might finally open up now, and tell her what he had been unable to tell her before. But all he did was give her a weird look, so she withdrew her hand and began to scrutinize her own fingers, while he went to his room and started picking out the *Star-Spangled Banner* again, with the same misses and the same halts.

Marta contemplated her outstretched hand and tried to recall her fingers the way they had been before the war started. The memory would not come, she was haunted all the time by the strange, hollow sound of the electric guitar coming from her boy's room, and she wished she was rid of it, rid of this sound. But she could not think of any way to make it happen.

She looked at the fingers on her hand. Had they changed? It seemed less and less impossible, and she became convinced that she had been wrong—that the fingers this boy had shown her were in fact not her boy's fingers from before the war. And maybe she was also beginning to think that her own fingers were not the same. But everything was so complicated already, she did not want to have to think about that as well. She just wished that this stranger, who could not find the right melody no matter how hard he tried, would move out of her house, so that her son could return.

It is evening again. Marta is sitting on the porch, nibbling cookies and gazing into the distance. She knows the next war is lurking there. She knows the next war will be a terrible war, a glorious war, a war that will right all wrongs, that will restore her son's fingers, and her son to her. And somewhere up there, somewhere in her son's body, something is playing a song that will sound right when this all happens.

He refused to be the same as them, although the offer was a good one. While waiting for the question he thought: Money can't compare to eternity because it's made to pass on. To pass on, that's it. It was possible that he would have become the same as them if they had not all gone before him, every one of them saying: "Same here." Had he not been last, he would have thought he did not stand a chance. Just like always. And it would not have mattered. But he *was* last, and he knew that he finally had his opportunity not to be the same. Forever. So he refused to play along. He spoke out.

The men standing by the back wall of the courtroom pushed their hands deeper into their raincoat pockets. Metallic clicking captured numbed, perplexed grins on faces. And before the gavel fell, everyone had grabbed their belongings, in a flap to get home and hide under the covers and pretend that the spoke in the wheel was just a bad dream and that news reports do not make dreams any more real even if they do appear in the late editions, the reporters having dropped their open pads and dashed to the phones.

The judge said: "You may step down," and a thin rivulet of sweat trickled from beneath his wig, his face shining in disbelief, in fear: What was this stunt now? What would be the upshot for him? For his wife? For his children? He glanced around the courtroom, but there was no way out, it had been audible, they had all heard it, so the judge must have heard it too. But to hell with it all (and there will be hell to pay), he was the judge, no other.

He, on the other hand, walked past the man staring at the floor, wedged between two police officers, the man whose face he knew down to the last pore, and everything felt infinitely easy. Words, it had only taken words, and here was eternity. As he stepped through the main entrance, he was blinded by sunlight, and he shaded his eyes with his hand and looked at the bustling crowd.

"Something's happened," the people cried and ran in all directions, tugging at the sleeves of passers-by and pointing at the sky, "something's finally happened, something has actually happened at last."

He fished a cigarette out of his pocket and started feeling around for his lighter, which must have slipped through a tear in the lining. He glanced over his shoulder, as though expecting one of the young men waiting in front of the building, leaning against the walls, to bring a hand out of his raincoat pocket, cupped around a lighter, but none of them moved.

I am not the same as them, he thought and joined the hustle and bustle, thinking about the tobacconist in the side street who must still have plenty of matches since hardly anyone passes by at this time of day. All the men in raincoats followed him, as though they too were craving a smoke. Now I truly stand no chance, he thought, of dying in the fashion of a Biedermeier picture: wrapped in a woolen shawl, reclining in a worn armchair, a grandchild in my lap.

ELECTRIC GUITAR

Hidden in the dusk, the boy tries over and over to pick out that miserable tune on the accordion. He can't do it. Not a single note forms a harmony with its predecessor; his fingers on the buttons sometimes reach too low, then too high, and every time the bellows bleat out a jarring discord. The boy is not very musical, but he knows enough to realize that his goal—to play the simple air correctly—is becoming increasingly unattainable with every passing moment, just as the time when his father will return, and demand to be played to, is drawing inexorably nearer.

The night descends upon him like a damp cloth. The dense clusters of music printed on the sheet first begin to blend, then disappear altogether in the dark. The boy does not turn on the light, as the dark brings some relief; it is awful to watch his fingers stumbling over one another in such helpless confusion. Now he can only hear them.

But he does not hear the awkward, elusive melody, only his own fingers refusing to obey. And he knows that once again he won't be able to make his father see that it's not his fault, it's his fingers that are to blame. The more he explains how hard he's tried to unravel the mystery of this tune, the more entangled he'll get and the clearer it'll become that he still doesn't know for certain what some of the symbols on the music sheets mean and that every now and then he leaves out a couple. His father will hear him out patiently, as he always does, but will already be pulling the belt out of his pants. And then he'll say: Go on, son, play it again.

And the boy will play it again and the tune will be even more jagged as his fingers leave sweat marks on the keys, making them slippery. And the father will listen and stroke his leather belt, and then he'll say: Son, put away the accordion.

The boy thinks about what is in store and tears well up in his eyes. The worst part is that he loves music. When he lies in bed at night, he shuts his eyes tight and imagines himself as that boy in a white tuxedo and bow tie he's seen on television, standing center stage in a concert hall, holding a violin in his hand and taking a bow while the audience applauds enthusiastically. His reality is different: His only audience is his father, and he doesn't clap for joy.

The boy knows what is wrong, he knows why he can't find the right notes. He's under the spell of the electric guitar. It's everywhere. It's got all the right sounds and won't let his accordion have a single one of them. It's got into his head and filled it with a white buzz that doesn't allow any rivals near. That's why his quaking tones can't flow together into a melody. They're not allowed to by the electric guitar. Only it can find the way. He saw that on television too. He saw how it had all started. Somewhere far away, somewhere in Africa, the devil played the guitar and cast such a spell on it that nobody but its owner could play it. Everyone else was struck by a thunderbolt. Burned to ashes. Made no more. And that's why guitars are so dangerous. And the electric guitar, the most powerful of them all, is the most dangerous. If you're not the right person for it, that is.

The boy thinks: If he had an electric guitar, a real one, then he could do it. He'd be the right person for it and he could play it without a single mistake, and his father would not take the belt out of his pants, but would open his arms and lift him up and tell him how proud he was of him and the audience would clap their hands and he would adjust his bow tie, press the violin against his white tux and leave the stage and go back to his room where the two toys would be waiting for him, the toys on which the dust settles relentlessly during the hours when he so desperately tries to find the right line over the black and white keys. And then he would put the violin away and play with them, the teddy bear on which his mother had pinned the note saying she was leaving but that she would come get him real soon, right away, and that she loved him, and the Barbie doll his little sister had left behind even though it was the one she talked to more than to anything else. And other toys, many other toys he does not have now.

The boy knows it's a fantasy. All his hours of reveries over the accordion are empty. The only thing real is the squealing box in his hands and the sheet on the music stand from which he cannot decipher the melody. And the electric guitar in his head. Which can play all the melodies and knows all the ways.

The boy wonders: How did his father guess the electric guitar was so dangerous? How did he know not to get him one when he asked for it? How did he know it would spew fire if it came into the hands of the boy? His father told him that this accordion was the very same one he himself had played, and his father and grandfather before him, and that there'd be no guitar in his house. He meant in his room, because they live in a room, not a house, but the boy understood anyway. And marveled. True, his father knows about music, he's forever bringing him new sheets and placing them on top of the ones the boy has gazed at to exhaustion. But how could he also know the secret of the electric guitar, which is hidden to all and has only been revealed to the boy?

Every time the boy told his friends how the electric guitar could bring back the dead and shake up the living so that not a trace of life remained in their bodies, they'd giggle and wink at one another, and then, when he fell silent and turned away, they whispered behind his back that he was a bit touched. Yes, he heard it quite distinctly: A bit touched. But he was never touched by anyone or anything except when his father touched him too hard, far too hard. He knew what the phrase meant: They thought he was a bit off. That there was something wrong with him. He clenched his fists and kept silent. And thought to himself: If I had an electric guitar I'd show them. They think an electric guitar's just a thing. A thing those who know how can make produce sounds. And that these sounds are no more than that: Just sounds. What do they know! They don't know that the electric guitar has a will and a life of its own, and that you have to be careful around it. Very careful.

The boy glances at the accordion in his hands, the cold, dead object which wheezes shapeless noises. He feels like flinging it on the ground and jumping up and down on it. Possibly, just possibly, that might give it some pep. But it would never become an electric guitar. Just as he—the boy knows, he—will never become that boy in the white tuxedo with the bow tie, on the concert hall stage, holding a violin in his hand and bowing while the audience claps effusively. And just as his father's belt will never become his mother's tarragon cake which she used to bake every Sunday when his father still let her out of the house to buy the groceries.

Over and over the boy grapples with the same shaky tune. He can't do it, he just can't do it. The keys evade him and the boy knows he won't make it. Somewhere in the corner, in the corner of the room, in the corner of his head, in the corner of the universe, there lurks the electric guitar.

Electricity gives power to all things, it's no wonder the boy can't manage without it. There's no music any more without electric power. It's no wonder his tunes are all squashed up and his fingers stumble over each other. I need an electric guitar, thinks the boy. Or at least electricity. It gives power to things.

Anxiously, the boy listens for sounds from the stairwell. For the time being he can't hear his father's heavy footsteps, but they will come before long. The boy knows that his father is seething with a rage he can barely control, and has been for a long time. The boy feels bad about it because he knows that his father loves him, and he has some idea how disappointed his father must be when he listens time and again to the boy hopelessly chasing after the melody. The boy remembers how often his father used to take him with him when he left home, and how they'd walk along the streets for hours on end and do nothing else, and how good it felt when his father put his arm around his shoulders. Except that one day when they came home and his mother and his little sister were gone, and only the teddy bear and the Barbie doll remained. And the note that said Mommy would come get him real soon. But she didn't. Not then and not later, though he waited.

His father explained to him that his mother and sister had left because women had no sense of duty, and that now they'd have to cope on their own. But the boy still felt that he and his father could have stayed on where they were and needn't have moved to another town, where his father enrolled him in a different school and where they had a different name on the door and his father called him a different name which he didn't like half as much as the one before, though he'd already forgotten what that was. Where they used to live, the apartment was bigger and the people were nicer. They'd often ask about his mother, about where she was, and they'd send their regards. Now there were no regards and nobody so much as knew that he'd ever even had a mother.

It occurs to the boy that the melody is unable to find its way out of the accordion. No, it won't work without power. He'll have to help the tune, it can't feel well, trapped in the choking bellows, it must want out, thinks the boy. Yes, electricity; the tune can't get out without power.

The boy finds the extension cord in the cupboard where his father keeps his tools. He turns over the accordion in his hands for a long time, unable to find an appropriate socket. First he blames it on the darkness, but finally it dawns on him that he's gone about it all wrong: It's the cord that needs to be changed to match the accordion, not the other way around. Using the knife he keeps under the pillow in case the dark man returns—the man who used to bend over him at night and breathe hot air on him until he screamed and screamed and screamed—he cuts the cord on the end which doesn't plug into the wall and strips apart every separate wire. Then, by touch alone, he attaches the individual wires to the frame of the accordion, until he feels they are all connected to something and that his work is done.

As he pushes the plug into the wall outlet, he hears a noise on the stairs. It's his father returning. He'll stumble on every step, then he'll be ever so long inserting the key in the lock, and the key will, as always, get stuck; then he'll get the door unlocked somehow, open it, and enter.

The boy knows what lies in store for him, and it paralyzes him; he forgets about the accordion, about the sheet music spread out on the stand, about the instant soup he was supposed to be stirring into boiling water this very moment because his father wants to eat when he comes home.

He squeezes into the gap between the wall and the closet, where he usually keeps his accordion, and hopes it will just go away, as it sometimes does. He hopes his father won't find the strength to listen to him play, that he'll just stagger over to bed and fall asleep without even kicking his shoes off. Then all the boy will have to do is cautiously remove them for him.

His father enters the room. He mutters indistinctly into his chin. He walks into the table, kicks over a chair with a crash. The boy presses further into the cranny, such a narrow space that his father, so he hopes, won't be able to follow. Because if he does, the boy knows, it's going to be bad. It will be unending.

Although the room is filled with darkness, the father spots the accordion on the floor. He grumbles something sharply and bends over to pick it up, but as he takes hold of it he shudders, starts shaking, throws his head back, does a little offbeat dance with an unusual rhythm, and this goes on and on. Then the accordion slips from his fingers, and when it hits the ground the bellows emit a muffled moan, as the father collapses on the floor. He drools.

The boy waits. It's an ugly sight, gross, but he's seen it before. The boy reasons that his father didn't make it to bed this time. That's happened before too; he doesn't always make it. And so he doesn't need to take his shoes off either since there's no bed linen to get dirty.

The father does not move for a long time. The boy contemplates his next step. Usually, his father groans after a while, murmurs, yells. But nothing this time. Nothing. He lies motionless, still. The boy begins to realize it's different this time. And he doesn't know what to do.

At last he creeps out of his hiding place, unplugs the cord and puts it away, back into the cupboard. His father is always telling him to put things away; if you don't, you get covered with grime and dust, you need to put things away, be neat and tidy, scrub the dirt and dust off your body. And then he scrubs the dust off the boy's body for a long, long time until the boy shivers under the spray of cold water since all the warm water has long been used up, and then his father picks him up and carries him to bed and draws his hand over his eyelids so that they close and then the boy can feel his father looking at him for a long, long time, and the boy knows that his father wishes him a good night and sweet dreams, and no dark man or hot breath on his cheek.

The boy looks at his father for a long, long time, but still the father does not budge. The boy thinks. He can't stay like this forever, he thinks. Finally he takes the keys out of his father's breast pocket. Although it sometimes takes his father a long time to locate the lock, he is always quick to put the keys carefully away. Always. The boy had already tried to open the door when he was home alone, to open the door and go to Africa to get the guitar, but he never once could find the keys. And the windows were so high up he got dizzy when he looked through them at the bottomless abyss beneath.

The boy stands on the staircase and hesitates. His heart sinks because it is very dark already, and even if it were daylight, he does not know the way. There's not a single way he knows, because his father always accompanies him whenever he needs to go out, or go to school. But the boy knows he has no choice. There's only one option: He must find his mother. He'll ask on the corner if somebody knows her. He remembers her name, he's repeated it to himself over and over since she left, leaving behind that note. Somebody's bound to know her. If not on this corner, then on the next one or on the one after that; there is always at least one more corner. Sooner or later he'll find her. He knows he must. He must find his mother. She'll know what to do next, she'll explain what happened. And maybe, just maybe, she'll let him talk her into buying him an electric guitar.

Hello, Father. Do you remember? I'm here, waiting. Do you remember me? A whole lot has come to pass, but I haven't forgotten about you. I verified the communications. And believed that it really was the way you said it was. So there. I learned the language and made notes on the walls. I murmured your name when there were no others.

It's true: I've been there. In the heart of the matter. As you said. Over and over. I was what you wanted. I did not fend off fate. I did not try it on for size. I thought of you and waited.

I was Črtomir. I stood on the edge of the precipice, my hands clasped high above me; somewhere far away centuries went by. I talked and I talked. In the background: My country in ruins. People evaporated, worlds sank into darkness.

I was the lovely Vida. I stood by the sea, waiting for my Moor to return. But he did not come. I waited a long time. Men walked by, offering me their semen. I kept declining for a long time. And waited.

I was Copernicus. I lay on the ground and listened to the world rotate. I considered crying out: Halt! Stop! I probably would have cried out if I could have. But I did not. I could not. My throat was dry. Arid. So many years without juice.

I was a painter. The crazy artist. I lived in a forest of sunflowers. By myself. The knife blade went through the ear tissue smoothly. It was like slicing butter. I felt faint, drank a glass of wine, got back on my feet again, then I started looking for wrapping paper. I was in a hurry, the post office was closing at six. It dripped through the paper, but there was no other way.

I was Antigone. I waited for my brother to dig his way out of the grave. I told him: Wash death from your face, my brother, and make this country merry again. Then everything will be different. My brother. Let them slay your sister. My brother looked at me, he looked at me for a long time.

I was a warrior. Hitler. And Mussolini. And the other one, what's-his-name, I forget what he was called. They cried out to me: Long live! Of course I heard the reverberations of goose-steps. Coming closer and closer. But I did not have time to run away. There was a war, a wonderful war, a good war. I awaited my fate. I knew it was coming. I brushed my uniform. I wanted to be ready when the door opened. I watered the plants and waited.

I was Tito, the victorious commander of poorly lit battlefields. They let me in the room, but I was not allowed to sit at the table. It was a large table, oblong, irregular in shape, not a table yet, actually, but some kind of fetus of a table. Marx, Stalin, and Mao played cards on it. I looked over their shoulders. The trumps kept changing: Now the sickle took them all, then the hammer. On the floor before the deep-freeze there was a pool of blood. I wanted to yell, but they all looked at me and put their fingers to their mouths.

I was what you wanted, Father. Dear Father. You never kept in touch. You never called. You never wrote. I had to fend for myself. And I did. I thought of you. I worked for you. What is done is done now. It all seems some sort of game. By who with whom I don't know. Not who, whom or where. That which is seems real. At least for the time being. It is. And I also. I am here now. I am.

Me and you, Father. Father. Are you there? Are you listening? I'm tired, Father. I can't tell your stories any more. I've forgotten my own. Can you hear it, can you hear it softly pulsating?

I don't want any more, Father. Too much is possible. Like in a dream. Someone dreams of waking up. Someone dreams of falling asleep. Someone dreams of dreaming. Someone sits in his room playing a complex game in which whole universes disappear, and is bored to death. Too many options, Father. I want a single one, so that there is no choice. So I cannot choose wrongly.

I am here. I feel. I dream. I breathe. Are you waiting? What are you doing? Where do you live? Are you coming?

Nora's Face

In 1904, James Joyce and his wife Nora traveled to Trieste, where he was to take a teaching post. They got off the train too soon and had to spend a night in the park near the Ljubljana railroad station.

I watch the man as he asks questions. He leans close to the ticket window. The silhouette on the other side, indistinct, unrecognizable, an extra in history, shakes its head. The man, bent into a sort of question mark, is disgruntled. He pounds on the counter. Somewhere beyond the edge of the picture there puffs a train. The man points in its direction. The shape behind the window keeps shaking its head. No, sir, I'm very sorry, sir, but there are no trains for you; this, this maybe.

A line forms behind the man, a line that does not move on. They are all waiting to begin their journeys, anxious to say what they want; why is this man holding us up, this man who speaks such a difficult language to understand? And I, knowing the story, smirk at the thought that it will be none other than this man who becomes a teacher. Even after a whole eternity has gone by, it will still be possible to speculate where to put a comma, where a semicolon, in his work; he'll never say it definitely once and for all, he'll beat about the bush, he'll dodge the issue. It's no wonder he missed the train, just as it's not a surprise that he got off it too soon. Yes, such a story is quite possible.

Now the man has squared his shoulders, squared them too much. I can tell he's trying to convince himself and the rest of the world that he's got the situation under control. That he knows where he is and what he's doing here. But if nothing else, it's his skin that gives him away. His translucent, pale skin, which can barely stand the strain of being stretched over the frame of bone, speaks of his coming from a different world. A world where sows eat their farrows. That's why he left. So that he wouldn't be eaten. And now he's here. In a town whose very name he ignores. A town in which there's nothing for him to do. And which he can only leave in the morning, and there's still a whole eternity until then.

The man bends to the woman sitting next to a suitcase. A young woman, looking at him as a wife does at the husband she has wanted her entire life and also wants the very next moment. (Yes, this is the way it would be written in a novel the man would refuse to read.) The man points to the ticket window; he makes a deprecating gesture. The woman, pouting slightly, shakes her head. The man points to the door, to the outside. The woman turns around, but not all the way, just a half-turn. Then her look returns to him. She nods, the man picks up the suitcase and starts for the door.

I know: Now, now she's making her mind up. If she does not follow him, I'll go ahead. I'll explain what's what to her. If it turns out this way, let him leave and let her stay. He won't be coming back; once he's outside, away from people, I'll get him entangled in a street fight or something. There's nothing easier to describe than the flash of a blade the moment before it scrapes against a rib. He'll like that. Perhaps, if he could choose or dream his own death, this would be the death he would choose or dream. It's going to be easy. He'll take a firm grip on the knife he has no idea how to handle. Very easy. I've done it before.

But the woman rises; she follows him. No, it won't work out the way I figured. I'll have to find another way. A different one. I ponder my next move. I could seek out the answers to his questions. I could give him anything he might want. Another train for Trieste, in a few minutes' time, in just as long as it takes to stroll across the tracks to the platform. Other places, other times. The Paleozoic. A world war. A quiet hour at tea time. Anything. A few combinations on the little machine I carry around with me would suffice. A few right connections on the screen, and everything's possible. New worlds emerge from the pulsating liquid crystal. Worlds where this young man could feel at home.

I'm in a quandary. I look around as if the surroundings might suggest a course of action. But everything is as usual—there's nothing much to see. Perhaps the appearance of this part of town has been planned to force one to leave. Just imagine: If the route to the exit were the most gorgeous thing in the world, who would actually want to go? This environment, though, spurs on even the undecided, making departure the best option.

I come here often. I watch. I think of places I could go. Some day. I'm in training. I practice a lot. On my machine. I buy all the new software. Since it keeps changing incessantly I assume the world also keeps changing. Though that's not plainly visible from here. There's always grass (it's always green), a few benches, then the sliver of the street, and the bustle on the far side. I never look across. That would be too much like leaving. I presume that people on the other side leave because they simply can't find their way back. Perhaps there is no way to get back.

I wonder whether the man is waiting. Let him wait, I tell myself. Every second millions of small, inconspicuous events occur. Worlds are born, planets crumble. And other things, an infinity of other things.

I watch the woman. He creates her according to the image of his desire. He'll write to her to tell her what kind of lingerie to buy. It'll work, too, it'll work out. This story will remain. It will be better than mine. More precise, more undefinable.

I know: In the future, when he speaks about his life, this young man won't say a word about tonight. Or about me. Or about the city on whose pavement we are both standing, listening to the city's muffled noise. Although his words will contain, without exaggeration, *the whole world*. I see now: With such a recording, the city, which is now shrouded in darkness and thus entirely at the disposal of my imagination, would begin to transform into something real, and it's common knowledge that reality is less malleable to the laws of our desires than are the figments of our imagination.

My story has run its course, my energy's ebbing, I'll have to finish. I thought of finishing before, but I felt it necessary to tell it all, through to the end. I only go out in the streets at night now. They're too dangerous in the daytime, sleeping, not showing their souls, nor the beating of their hearts. At night, however, a hot magma bubbles under the cold icing of sidewalks and streets, and sometimes when there's no-one near, it spurts through a pore in the asphalt and licks my face for a moment, just for a moment; then everything goes back to the way it was before. I love this city, I'm not going to leave it, although I'm told there are others too, some of them even closer than I thought.

I know this story cannot last. I've lived down there, under the top layer, so I know: The sewage does not drain anymore. It accumulates. The city only grows, feeding on its waste. And some day it will go off on its own way.

What else is there to tell? Sometimes, sometimes I seem to see Nora's face among the silicon dummies in store windows. I rush there, but, as you know, the faces change like holograms—what you see depends on where you watch them from. And I can never again find the spot from which I'd seen Nora's face. Then I press my lips to the glass and for a long time taste the traces of neon rain.

No

In the moment which lapsed between him raising his hand and it landing on her face she thought: Maybe it won't be so bad. Maybe all I have to do is think of something else and it'll blow over, just like that, nice and easy.

When her head was knocked sideways and her mouth filled up she knew she'd been wrong. She opened her mouth to speak but only produced a gurgle; only when she spat out once, twice, could she form words again.

I don't want to be with you. I don't. I'll go away.

No.

Yes, I will.

No, you won't.

He grabbed her by the throat. She thought—this is the end. Now he'll start squeezing and he won't be able to stop. I know him. He won't be able to stop—it'll be stronger than him.

She could see the skin on his wrist turn white.

No, she said. No, no, no.

His eyebrows drew together, his grip eased, and his eyes met hers.

Do you love me?

Now? she gurgled. Now?

Yes, now. Why should now be different from any other time?

The image in front of her eyes slowly began to recede. As though dissolving in water. The colors faded, the contours wavered. That's true—why should it? she thought. It's the same now as always. No difference at all. And love has to be the same.

Love, he said, leaning toward her, love is what matters.

Let go, she said, let go. And listened to her words turning into mush. I can't, like this.

He leaned closer.

Can't hear you, he said. Speak up. I can't hear you.

She wanted to repeat it, but she'd run out of air.

Do you remember, he said, speaking very softly himself, the time we first met?

She wanted to nod, she wanted to say: Sure I remember. How could I forget?

I remember everything, he said. I remember like it was yesterday. It wasn't yesterday though.

No, she thought, it's been a long time.

We've had some good times together, he said, very slowly.

Let go, she thought, let go.

Some good times indeed, he repeated. I wonder now where we went wrong.

Wrong? she thought. Did we go wrong? I don't want to die over some mistake I can't even remember. Maybe we never went wrong. Maybe this stage is the norm after all these years, except that most people can control themselves, they can hold back. To think of all the times I watched you at night, sleeping, breathing, and imagined how easy it would be to slit your throat. So easy. Except that I always told myself: You're crazy to harbor such thoughts. But maybe I wasn't crazy. Maybe I should've done it.

With his other hand he grabbed her T-shirt and yanked her to him. She could hear the fabric rip.

Automatically she raised her arms to shield her breasts. Then she realized how ridiculous the gesture was. Any moment now it won't matter anymore, she said to herself. But it was stronger than her. She covered her breasts with her hands and thought one more time: No. No, no, no.

Recognize the beginning, MM?

The day is hot, downright sweltering. Everything on earth is scorched. Leaves curl up and drop from trees, people limply drag themselves along, keeping close to the shelter of buildings, the town smells only of gasoline and dust. I stay in, as usual, sprawled out on my sweat-soaked bedspread and, using my forehead, wipe the condensation off another bottle of beer. I should take the tapes back to the video store, but moving about right now feels wrong. I should order a pizza, but I'm sure I'd be told that delivery has been canceled due to the weather. And they'd be right—who would light the oven for the sake of a single pizza in this heat? Single life is hard. I should get married, but it is too hot, maybe I should take a shower—

The doorbell rings.

"Thanks, I don't need any detergent!" I yell. Unless you start using it immediately, I think to myself.

The doorbell rings again.

"I have quite enough books, too," I try again. Which is an understatement. Not quite enough—books are becoming a considerable problem for me.

"It's me," a faintly familiar voice pipes up.

I rise and carefully step over the empty beer bottles all around the bed. The door is surprisingly far away, given I only possess twenty-six square meters of space.

It's Peter.

"You of all people," I say.

He recoils nervously. "Why do you say that?" he asks.

I close my eyes for a moment and take a deep breath. "That's alright. It's just hot. Grab a beer from the fridge and join me." I retrace my steps to the bed and drop back on it.

He goes to the kitchenette.

"I don't have a bottle opener," I call to him. "You have to hook the cap on the edge of the sink and slam the bottle."

There is a clatter, followed by a pathetic slap. I get up and go to the kitchen. Peter is standing there with a beer bottle in his hand, looking at it worriedly. I grab the bottle, open it with an expert swipe and return to the room. He slowly follows.

I don't have any chairs. Even if I wanted to waste money on them, I wouldn't know where to put them. I indicate the bed, but he shakes his head with a trace of disgust on his face. He sits on the floor with his back to the wall, his legs curled under him. I have never been able to understand what Tina sees in him; that's just the way women are, I suppose.

We drink. We hear muffled voices coming from the floor below. Peter scowls. My downstairs neighbor has a new girlfriend. They make out every day. Well, she's not brand new anymore. I already know precisely when it is going to end and how they are going to get there.

"Downstairs," I say. "My neighbor. If they lie lengthwise, the bed bangs against the wall. She's going to enjoy it today, I think."

"Jesus," he says.

I nod seriously. The sighing starts.

"What did I tell you," I wink at Peter.

"Jesus," he says again, more quietly this time as though he is straining his ears to hear. "Can't you put a stop to this somehow?"

I'm not certain he's serious. "Put a stop to it? How? Why?"

"I mean, the noise and all that—"

"Oh, that! What can you do, there are some things that just can't be done quietly."

He looks at me in desperation.

"Okay, don't let's waste any more time, you must be in a hurry. Why are you here?"

Peter presses his back to the wall. The sighs beneath him begin to fall into a rhythmic sequence. He lifts the bottle and tips it back. The bed down below starts creaking.

"My god," he says, "are they always this noisy?"

"It's not going to last long."

My neighbor grunts. The woman's voice calls out incomprehensible words. The banging of the bed against the wall is getting stronger.

"Now," I say.

We hear prolonged gasping and panting. Then everything falls quiet.

"See, what did I tell you? Now a shower and that's it. He'll fall asleep and she'll leave. How are things with Tina?"

"Tina . . . Fine, fine. Oh, god . . ."

I look at him. In the light seeping through the drawn blinds he looks as though vapor were rising from his face. He leans back on his elbows and stares at me grimly.

"Tina," he says, "is just great. Never better. But . . ."

This looks like it's going to take longer than the job downstairs. I put down my empty bottle and go for another one. When I return, he takes the initiative.

"How are things with you?" he says.

I shrug. "It's so darn hot."

"Financially, I mean."

A low blow, below the belt.

"I'll manage," I say. "I'll be rich if I get a refund on all these bottles. And sell my books, of course."

He glances around, as though trying to assess whether I'm joking.

"Do you get work?"

"I do, I do," I nod apprehensively. "Can't keep up at all. The phone's ringing off the hook, people are coming in droves . . ." I gesture vaguely; he looks at me with mounting disbelief.

"If you need any money . . ." he starts slowly.

"You might be able to help out? Would you like me to kill someone for you?" I say with an enthusiasm which is not entirely feigned.

"Just what I need," he mutters.

"Why did you come?" I say. "To borrow a book? No offence, but no go. I think you still owe me my copy of the Kama Sutra."

"The Kama Sutra?" he is startled and starts shaking his head vehemently. It's downright embarrassing.

"It was a joke," I admit with contrition. "Forgive me."

He shrugs and glares at his empty bottle, then at me. I nod encouragingly. He puts it down with the others, as there is nowhere else, and goes to fetch another. I listen to his attempts to knock off the cap. It takes him quite a long time.

I drink and observe him. I hardly know him. Tina got married while Monika and I were still in India. In one of those places where mail is not delivered. What was I supposed to do? When I returned, she had been hitched four months already. I studied Peter whenever we got together, and I never knew what to make of him. As long as Tina does, I told myself. Like hell she did. Once, we got drunk together at some family function, and she admitted she hoped Peter and I would get along well, seeing we were more or less the same age. Then I could tell her how to get along with him.

"So?" I say.

He decides to take the plunge.

"Do you think she's got another guy?" he asks and seems about to put a hand over his mouth.

"Who do you reckon she had before this one then?" I ask nonchalantly. I'll teach you to ask me if I have enough money!

He does not appreciate my wit.

"Oh, come on," he says. "We're both adults . . ."

"One more adult, the other less," I say. Mean, I admit.

". . . and the most adult of all is Tina."

I ponder his words. In all truth this cannot be denied. I have to concede the point.

"And yet—" he says. And falls silent. And yet—what? What non-adult thing could she have done now? This is becoming intriguing.

"What makes you think she's seeing someone else?" I ask tentatively.

Peter draws his head between his shoulders.

"You know how it is. I don't actually know all that much about her. I mean—what she was like before. Before me she had other—"

"This I absolutely do know," I own up.

He becomes embarrassed.

"Well, naturally. Otherwise we wouldn't be here talking."

Otherwise I would be spared all manner of things. I make a world-weary face.

"Whatever—" he says and pauses dramatically.

"I'm listening."

"Tina doesn't sleep at home any more."

Well, this could indeed be called a piece of news. Tina never— *never ever*—wanted to go places. She was distraught when I left for India. According to her, the world became sinister, insecure, predatory the moment you left your block. She stuck to home, she found that safest.

"Where does she sleep?" I ask.

Peter spreads his arms theatrically. "I have no idea. She comes home in the morning—"

"Well, at least she still comes home, that's not so bad, and it shows she's well brought up." I'm trying to give him courage. It doesn't work. He glances toward the kitchenette gloomily. I'll run out of beer before nightfall again, I think.

"And what does she say?"

"Nothing. She sleeps the whole day and then in the evening she goes out again . . ."

"So?"

Peter looks at me in surprise. "So—what?"

"I mean, does this bother you or what?"

"Sure it bothers me! I'm not used to this kind of thing. This didn't used to happen—"

"Life expectancy used to be shorter, and monogamy was easier to put up with."

Peter sighs. "I wasn't referring to *that* far back."

"Tell me something, Peter, and be honest."

He flinches. He did not expect such an opening. He expected me to send him packing, or at best, to the store to get more beer. But not this.

"Go ahead."

"Do you really miss Tina? Or are you just a little bored?"

He does not hesitate for a moment. "I really miss her."

Naturally, what was I thinking?

"Now you tell me something, and be honest," he's making the most of this opportunity.

I look at him archly, as if to say: Haven't I been the only one who *always* told you *everything* honestly?

"Shoot."

"What has your solitude done for you?"

Ha, so the gentleman is considering changing his marital status!

"Plenty," I retort.

"Name two things." Obviously I'm frowning pretty badly, because he amends it almost in the same breath: "One thing then."

"Sure, I could name things. More than one." Stop shooting your mouth off, I scold myself. You'll have a hard enough time coming up with one thing. "Since I've been living on my own, plenty of things have become clear."

"Like what?"

"Like some of the constants in folklore."

"Such as?"

"Like: All those animals which turn into princesses in fairy tales are the result of experiments with bestiality on lonely farms."

Now Peter frowns. "What are you talking about?" he says. He utters the words very slowly, as though he is afraid that I too will fail to understand him.

"Forget it," I say. "Want another beer?"

"I don't know."

I shrug and go to the fridge. To me it seems like one of the simplest questions a person could be asked on a late summer afternoon.

"Aren't you going to run out?" he calls after me.

"Sometime, definitely," I murmur. I proffer the bottle, and when he reaches for it, I draw my hand back. "Are you sure you know what bestiality is?" I say.

Peter looks around him, at the books, back at the bottles. "No, I'm not. I'm not sure," he says quietly.

"That figures." I toss the bottle in his lap and he seems relieved when it doesn't break. He looks at me in apprehension.

"Sexual intercourse with animals," I say.

It's clear Peter is beginning to feel queasy.

"Please don't go on," he mutters.

"There's nothing to go on about," I say. "That's it."

He shifts the bottle from hand to hand, wondering what comes next.

"Cheers," I say. With a gesture I demonstrate what he's supposed to do with the object he is cradling in his hands: Place the opening lower than the bottom and it works.

"I don't understand why she left," he does his best to change the subject.

"Left? You just said she comes back in the morning!"

"I mean, why she began leaving."

This philosophical turn in the discussion gives me a thirst. I consider another bottle, or rather the *idea* of another bottle, because I remember from my last trip to the fridge that I have in fact run out of booze.

"Maybe she wasn't getting hers anymore. You're old for her."

"Oh, please! I'm younger than you."

"That doesn't mean a thing. I'm old too."

Peter's patience is running thin.

"Why do you always have to be such a smart-ass? What's in it for you?" he raises his voice.

"Not much," I say modestly. "But I do know what bestiality is."

"And you've got books," adds Peter, somehow vindictively.

I nod contritely. "Do you want some?"

"I have plenty of problems without them," says Peter.

I see an opportunity for vengeance and I pounce on it. "Problems, right; while she took care of you everything was okay, but now that she wants to make up for lost time, you call it 'problems', do you? Why don't you enjoy the solitude like I do, my dear?"

The 'my dear' has a terrifically insulting ring, but he fails to notice.

"Listen—" says Peter.

I listen.

"I mean—the sexual revolution's over, right? You don't just run around having sex with everyone you happen to like, right? Or is it different again? Have I missed something? Do any of your books say anything about it?"

Whoever can use irony will live, I reason, so there's no point in sparing him.

"It seems to me that as far as you're concerned, the revolution was over the moment you snagged your broad, if you ever were part of it in the first place," I begin. "It's all right, I understand, the surrogate mother and all that."

He makes a face, a sure sign I'm on the right track. Of course, it's the same as always: As soon as I feel myself winning, I lose interest.

"Oh, let's drop it," I say and he nods passionately. "Since you're here . . . Have you made any progress with your guitar or is that riff from *Satisfaction* still the only thing you can play?"

He begins flexing his fingers in confusion. "The other day I caught something from *You Can't Always Get What You Want . . .*"

"Do you feel like a duet?" I motion toward the corner where both my guitars are propped. "The acoustic or the electric one?"

His eyes glitter. I rarely let him have a go at my electric guitar. "Can I use my own pick?"

I nod and he pulls out some piece of driftwood. I know I'm about to be regaled with an extreme solo on one string, but what can you do, even at my place guests have certain privileges.

"What shall we play?" I ask, taking the acoustic guitar in my hands. They both need tuning, I have not played them separately for a long time, let alone together, but there's no point in wasting time.

"Can you do the classic, E A E B seventh?"

"I think I could if I put my mind to it," I say with reservation.

"But before we start, tell me what you're going to do about Tina?"

Just holding the electric guitar does wonders for his self-confidence. He grins.

"Worried I'll walk out on Mommy and make her miserable, are you? Play, you spoiled kid."

Okay, I think, it seems you've got your act back together again. And Tina's old enough to fend for herself. And besides, who am I to get involved in her affairs, deciding what's right and wrong?

I start playing and he's immediately off into a solo. Naturally, he gets lost before we get to the seventh the second time around. I hope you're having a good time at this moment, Tina, I think, while I hopelessly try to keep up with his improvisation. Because my stepfather and I are not doing so great.

Peter stops in the middle of the riff, as is his wont. The thought crosses my mind that it is becoming increasingly clear why Tina will not sleep at home anymore.

"Listen—" he says.

"I am listening," I grumble, "But we're not doing so hot."

He twitches impatiently and the guitar twangs with the best sound so far.

"No, no, not that," he says. "I wanted to ask you—do you know any interesting women?"

Hmm, it seems he's trying to cash in on the generational bond and all that. I think of my neighbor's new girlfriend.

"I didn't know my stepfather was interested in women," I parry haughtily. "And I didn't know he considered me depraved enough to assist him in his adulterous thoughts and intentions."

He grimaces. Of course, it does not escape his notice that I have not attributed any adulterous acts to him.

"I didn't know my stepson was all grown-up now and an ardent supporter of exemplary family life." He tries to get even to the best of his ability. "A sign of the times!"

"Indeed," I murmur and strum out a few chords from *Brown Sugar*. He does not pick them up. Perhaps the piece is too difficult for him.

"Don't you like my musical selection?" I ask tentatively. Yes, my guess has been correct, his scowl reveals he had hoped for something different.

"I don't understand why we always have to play The Stones and nothing else," he says, looking at the floor as though he is embarrassed.

"Don't you like them? The tradition, the lore passed down to us by our forefathers?"

"I like them alright, it's not that, it's just—"

Peter uses pauses the way some people underline words in a letter when they wish to give them meanings they do not inherently possess. I wait.

". . . it's just somehow they don't belong to our time."

I lifted my shoulders. "What do you want us to play, then? Do you want me to get my records from the age of disco? Then we can scratch if I can get hold of a record player someplace."

"I think we should look forward, not backward."

I can barely contain myself from screaming at the pomposity of his words. All his bewilderment notwithstanding, Peter has always been a bit too big for his breeches. I suppose that was what Tina liked. In the beginning, anyway.

"And what should we play in that case?"

"Not these . . . stories of dissatisfaction. The Stones, punk rock . . . That's old hat. It's time for something new. Something that would bring people together."

Stories of dissatisfaction! Where did he get that? The situation is becoming quite comical. If everything else fails in my life, I think, I can spend the rest of my days in comfort at the thought of Peter founding some political party or religious sect and saving the world.

"Time for love songs?"

The idea does not strike Peter as totally bizarre, he does not detect the irony; on the contrary, it seems he would find a thing like that refreshingly new.

"Why not," he says, absolutely seriously. "Don't you think we could do it?"

"Do you have anything specific in mind?"

If he suggests *I Just Called to Say I Love You* or some similarly corny sop, I'll throw him out, I tell myself.

No, he does not have anything specific in mind. "Let's just improvise," he says.

Of course, he cannot actually play anything and he hopes I'll take longer to spot his mistakes this way. And who am I to raise objections now, who am I to spoil his fun, when the man is obviously convinced he's on the right track?

"Peter," I say.

"Yeah?" He expects me to say no improvisation, The Stones or nothing. But I am not going to say that.

"About those interesting women, Peter—"

"Yeah?"

"They keep passing my window, here."

At first Peter looks at me in surprise, staring vacuously for a while, then he grins.

"So that's why you never go out? I get it."

If you understand anything, please explain it to me too, I think. But I do not say it, and we plunge into improvised love songs without lyrics, or some such noodling. Peter looks happy, the electric guitar resounds louder and louder. My downstairs neighbor starts banging on the ceiling.

Why don't you come up and join us, I think, and next time I'll join you, there are some things that just can't be done quietly. And we play on. And it begins to seem to me that it's better without words.

TOTAL RECALL

Liza writes with a thin felt-tip pen on the wall of the club toilet. The wall vibrates with the beats of the bass drum, and the syncopated rhythm distorts her otherwise delicately drawn letters into wobbly squiggles. She could do with a sturdier pen, her inscription will be hard to notice amongst the numerous others covering the walls. But as she did not know in advance that she was going to write something, she did not come prepared; all she had with her was the felt-tip pen she occasionally uses to jot down a note in her diary. Never mind. What's important is that it writes. This is not why she went to the bathroom, oh, no, she went because she had to go.

But as she crouched awkwardly above the toilet bowl (which she absolutely must not touch, she told herself incessantly, because everybody sits on it and it's absolutely crawling with filth) and looked at the other writings on the stall wall, it seemed everything was written there except for the most vital thing of all. The crucial thing: Her story. And she felt she had to change that. There's no rush; her girl-friends, who are all huddled around one of the little tables in a corner, can wait. They'll just go on lying to one another anyway, about the way they ostensibly spent last night, about the films they haven't in reality seen, about the gifts they haven't gotten, about the cars in which they haven't ridden, about the boys they haven't kissed, and from time to time they'll exchange glances and one of them will say: "I say, Liza's taking a long time!" and then they'll giggle for a long time as though it was all so funny.

I got AIDS from Mark Novak.

This is what Liza is penning. She is almost done, which is just as well because the felt-tip pen is running out of juice, just as she is running out of strength. Every single letter makes her feel weaker, every new letter makes her wish harder she hadn't gone out with her friends, at least not tonight, and also not that time when she met Mark Novak in this same club, and also not all those other nights when she said at home she was going out with her friends and in turn told her friends she was staying at home, while in reality she was going out with Mark Novak. Though never to this club, not once, because she was never absolutely certain that one or the other of her friends would not already be here, or even all of them, who would then put their heads together and start giggling when one of them said something Liza could not catch, and then would go on giggling for a long time as though it was all so funny.

Liza does not actually have AIDS. But she did not know that for certain until today, when she got her test results back. Ever since the moment Mark told her he had another girlfriend—or rather not *another girlfriend*, since that would mean that she had been his girlfriend—but from the moment he told her he was *seeing someone*, from that moment she was convinced she had AIDS. And she did not know what to do at first. Should she take a test or just start saying good-bye to the world? So, unable to decide, she did both. Saying good-bye to the world proved to be a piece of cake. Going to the clinic for the test was harder. It was a form of confession that you were doing it. That you were—(Liza closes her eyes and presses her lips together as she says the words in her mind, but at least now she can say them, she couldn't do it at first, then she practiced a lot, every night, by herself, almost until morning)—*getting laid*.

There were other words for it, plenty of them. Even tonight, in this place, at the table her friends had all squeezed around when the DJ put on a slow number and none of the cool guys came to ask them to dance, they had used more words for it than Liza could handle. That's why she said she had to go, and ran to the bathroom. But not fast enough to avoid hearing one of them say to all the others and—at least that's the way it seemed to Liza—to the whole world: "There, you see, Liza's gotta go too!" Then they giggled as though it was all so funny.

Liza writes with a thin felt-tip pen on the wall of the club toilet and remembers. She recalls the damp smell in that hallway, and how she kept turning her head toward the door, afraid it would open, and how she strained her ears every time footsteps approached and then retreated. She recollects the coldness of the wall and then the stone floor, she recalls how chilly Mark's hands were on her skin, she recalls he was so close she could smell the beads of sweat on his face, she recalls how he pulled her panties off her and how she pulled them back on, but not firmly enough, obviously not firmly enough because then they were off, down there somewhere, on the floor, lying somewhere far away, a patch of white in the dark. And she recalls most of all how she just kept waiting for it to be over, only hoping that some friend of hers didn't see her, see her and say: "Oh, look at her down there, under Mark Novak, I know her, that's Liza!" Say that and then giggle as though it was all so funny.

Actually, thinks Liza, I may've had it quite good with Mark Novak. It could have been worse; some of the girls who dared talk about these things told stories which to Liza seemed far worse. Mark picked up her clothes afterwards and dusted them off; Mark gave her a hand up; after, Mark said they'd go for a soft drink or a coffee; Mark said okay, some other time then, when she said she couldn't go for a soft drink or a coffee because she had to go home straight away; Mark said he'd call, though he didn't, but at least he *said* he would—she heard from her friends that some guys didn't even say it, let alone call, and she also felt that some guys really were like that, maybe nearly all of them were, except Mark. And she thought it was really strange that when they were talking about this, her girlfriends giggled as though it was all so funny.

It occurs to Liza that actually she shouldn't be doing this, that actually she shouldn't be writing on the wall, not this inscription. Because whoever takes this seriously will think that what's written is true, that Mark Novak is HIV-positive, and then they'll feel that they have to do something about it, that they have to put him away or something, and she'd hate that, that's not what she wants, no, she really doesn't want that, not only because she's not sure that Mark

Novak has AIDS, not only because she actually thinks that Mark Novak does not have AIDS, but because if he had it, thinks Liza, he would act totally differently. If he had it, he surely wouldn't have taken her to that hallway, he surely wouldn't have kissed her, leaning against that cold wall, not Mark Novak, that's for sure, maybe some of the guys her friends talked about would, but not Mark Novak, thinks Liza.

And if Mark Novak sees this inscription, thinks Liza, it's possible he'll know straight away who wrote it, that it was her, Liza, thinks Liza, because Mark Novak may not know another girl who could have gotten AIDS from him. Because, thinks Liza, Mark Novak could've just *said* that he was *seeing someone*, while in reality that *someone* didn't exist, there was just her, Liza, and he spoke about *someone* just because he wouldn't admit to himself, and much less to Liza, that in reality he only had one girl, just her, just Liza. She could ask her friends about Mark Novak, she could ask them if they knew about him and some other girl, if there was any other girl at all. She could just ask them all that, casually, no problem, they ask each other stuff like that all the time. She could ask them alright, but only if she hadn't gone to that damp hallway with him. Now she can't, because she would blush in mid-question, or her voice would break; and if she blushed or her voice broke, one of them or maybe all of them would look her straight in the eye, stare into her eyes for a while and then hiss: "Why, Liza! Why do *you* want to know?" and then her friends would giggle as though it was all so funny.

Liza writes with a thin felt-tip pen on the wall of the club toilet, with tears trickling down her cheeks. Liza does not know what to do. She writes, although in reality she does not want to write. She wishes she had never taken the felt-tip pen out of her purse, that she had never gone to the bathroom. The thought crosses her mind that perhaps she should wish she had never come to this club, not tonight and not that night when she met Mark Novak here; or at least that she had never gone to that damp hallway, that Mark Novak could just go on being the boy who drinks soft drinks or coffee and cannot tell Liza from the rest of the girls, the boy her girlfriends talk about though he always looks away and will never notice Liza even though she looks at him a lot. It might have been better that way, it might have been even better if her girlfriends had noticed that she looked at him a lot and told her that they had noticed, and then giggled as though it was all so funny.

Liza spits on her writing and tries to rub it off, but her felt-tip pen appears to be waterproof and the writing will not come off the wall, all Liza manages to do is smudge the whole thing a bit so that it ends up looking as though it has been there a long time, as though it has not just been written by a girl who has just left the toilet. Liza flings her pen into the john, flushes and notices with horror the pen come floating back to the surface, so she flushes again and again with always the same result, the pen is still there, and then Liza throws lots and lots of paper on top of it and finally it goes down the drain. Then Liza washes her face with cold water and decides to return to her friends, to sit back on her seat and not start crying when one of them says: "Well, Liza! What took you so long in the bathroom?" and they all start giggling as though it was all so funny.

Liza makes her way back toward the dance floor and wonders why Mark Novak never comes to this club anymore, not since he told her that he was *seeing someone*. She wonders why he never comes together with that someone, so that Liza could see her and make sure that there really is this *someone*. Liza glances around, checking if Mark has come today and she's missed him in this bustle of bodies, among the flashes of light slashing the dark. Liza glances around, searching, but now there is nothing but the reverberating percussion, there is nothing but the neon stamps that are briefly imprinted on the bodies. Liza glances around and sees someone wave an arm, sending flying a spray of beer foam which strikes the wall and oozes down, and she sees someone notice and arch an eyebrow. Liza sees gathered in the corner those who no longer feel like moving, she watches their tongues touch, she watches a hand curve and float through the air to touch someone's face, she watches and remembers that damp hallway and she remembers the beads of sweat on Mark Novak's eyebrow and she recalls everything, she can recall absolutely everything. She remembers that hallway as though she had never left, and she recalls how it was and she knows it will never be any different from the way she recollects.

Liza makes her way back toward her friends and ponders. She thinks about telling them all about it, how it was in that damp hallway because, thinks Liza, it was an awful lot different from all the stories they pass around night after night, and, thinks Liza, maybe her friends don't actually know what it's really like, this thing and all, and they certainly don't know what it's like with Mark Novak, and maybe she should tell them everything about it, and when she stops telling them and they all look at her in surprise, wondering why she told them all that, this Liza who's always, but I mean *always*, so absolutely quiet, when they look at her in wonder and shake their heads, then Liza could start giggling as though it was all so funny.

The Day of Independence

This is the story Papa will tell me. Papa, who'll know for a long time to come how it was in the old days before you and me, when you could not accept a candy from a stranger in the street because it was poisoned for sure, when only strangers in the street had candies which you could not accept if you wanted to stay alive. This is a story from the end of that time and you have to hear it too, listen to it so that you can pass it on to your children when the time comes. That's why I'm confiding it to you, and we'll speak guardedly, *sotto voce*, choosing our words with care, as befits those days of old, and we'll glance over our shoulders in case there's somebody there, eavesdropping on what is none of their business.

He was there, Papa will boast, he was right there in the first few rows up front, and the cork which popped uncontrolled from one of the numerous bottles of champagne hit none other than him as he pushed his way to the platform, stretching a hard-won glass up to the scene, and the cork printed a blackish bruise above his eye. As accidents never come alone, in surprise he loosened his frantic grip on the glass, and it shattered on the ground, and Papa, stumbling, fell on his hand, and then, as soon as the people drew back enough for him to pick himself up, he saw the crisscross of blood on his palm.

There were a few screams, nobody had expected blood, not on a day they had been anticipating for so many years, generation after generation, lifetime after lifetime. They all knew it was possible though nobody had expected it to actually happen, but it happened, things like that do happen. It's alright though, no harm done, everybody around him said, so that in the end Papa said it too, what else could he do? It's alright, he said, and people laughed, patting his shoulders: it's okay, it's alright, they called out all around, while his palm dripped blood and hurt. It's alright, he said through clenched teeth, and kept repeating it, and then he accepted the proffered glass of brandy and downed it in one gulp, as fast as possible, and it really began to seem that it had to be alright since everybody said so, himself included, that there could be no harm, although his palm smarted strangely.

With the second glass it became crystal-clear to him that everything was indeed alright, really and truly. If there had been something that was not alright, it was before, but no longer now and never again, so he did not resist much when that girl started kissing him, it was totally acceptable, there was plenty of kissing going on all around, it was a special time like never before and possibly never again, and it's hard to hold back if everyone else is kissing, in particular if the girl does not even try to stop you, but quite to the contrary lays her hand on your bruise so often that the pain disappears and is replaced by another feeling, pleasant and unknown. And that's why Papa did not resist when this girl whispered to him that it was really too crowded here and that also here, in the old part of town—oh, not just a town anymore, as of tonight the capital—there were plenty of hidden corners which have been there since always, waiting since always for couples like them. And that's why Papa followed her, that's why he let her take him by the hand and lead him into one of those dark hallways whose reason for being might be that in them people can let out or shoot up fluids, into one of those hallways whose murky darkness screens out unwanted stares. And you know what happened in that hallway, things like that happen to everyone, or nearly everyone, in particular on days like that which had never happened before and will never happen again.

He doesn't remember much, Papa will tell me, he doesn't recall exactly what happened to him in that hallway, it was over so fast, faster than he expected or hoped, but it felt nice, pleasant, it felt the way it should on a special day, the kind of day one experiences for the first time, if one does at all, that is. Because it seems, Papa will go on, that there are also people to whom these things never happen, but such people, Papa will add, don't really know what they're missing, and so possibly they don't feel so bad about it as they would if they did know.

He does recall, though, Papa will also tell me, that when they picked up their things and went back outside, under the independent sky, a woman spoke to them, a woman dragging behind her several flattened cardboard boxes tied together with a piece of string. Excuse me, do you two live in a box, she asked, and Papa recalls shaking his head, he recalls looking into his woman's eyes and seeing them fill with horror. Then give me some change, the cardboard woman rejoined, and Papa recalls reaching into his pocket without hesitation, expecting to find something there, but there was nothing, he had left everything at the stands where champagne was served. Nothing was free, not even on a day like this—is anything ever free if nothing is free on a day like this? He recalls reaching into his pocket and not finding anything there, and his woman took him by the hand: No, no, she said, although he himself had also felt that no, that wouldn't do, even though he might have wished that it could have. And he recalls, Papa will finally tell me, how they went on together, he and this woman from the hallway, his woman for the night, with whom he was to become a couple, but not right away, not that night, oh, no, quite some time would go by, first they would circle around each other, pondering whether they should or should not, but then they found out about me and finally owned up that they were a couple, Papa will finish, and how they went on and how the cardboard woman followed them with her eyes for a long time, before she began arranging her cardboard boxes in the hallway, that hallway they had just vacated.

This is the story Papa will tell me when I ask how I came into this world, and he'll tell it to me softly, as though embarrassed about things being the way they were, about his palm bleeding and about not finding anything when he reached in his pocket. And I won't understand why he's embarrassed, just as you don't understand why

I'm embarrassed when I tell you this story, and just as your children won't understand you when the time comes for them to know about it.

But that is still far in the future, let's leave that for you to deal with when the time comes. Another story is about to happen, I can't hold back any longer, my day is coming. I'm about to enter the world, and I'll delight in the gust of air which will penetrate my body, it will be all different than it is inside here, it will be all unknown and large, dissimilar, and it'll be good, it can't be anything but good, and I'll scream for joy. The woman I'll later, much later, learn to call Mom will be there, gasping somewhere in the background. What is this? I'll ask myself, what's going on? Why doesn't this voice shut up? And Papa will lean close to me, he'll touch me, and I'll feel for the first time the raspy, cold skin which will be close to me so many times in the future. It will be an odd feeling, not unpleasant, just odd, when before that everything around me pulsated and gurgled, and now suddenly this. And he'll say something to me, but I won't understand what he's saying.

Papa. Papa. This is the way it's going to be, Papa. You'll come into my life, you'll be in it, and I'll devote a lot of time and effort to figuring out your stories. Stories from the old days without me, from a time when you could not accept a candy from a stranger in the street because it was poisoned for sure.

Just As Well

Thanks for the melody, SD

When the man returns from work earlier than usual, he finds his wife in bed. With his best friend, naturally. Ain't you two nice and cozy! What am I supposed to do? What do you do if a thing like this happens to you? he asks them, caught totally off guard. Of course, it immediately occurs to him, there's always that gun hidden in the closet, under the shirts, wrapped in an old T-shirt. When the army was leaving to go south, that sort of thing could be bought cheap, and so he decided to stock up, just in case, just like everyone in the know did.

The two of them, cringing grimly under a sheet with a dainty floral pattern, do not say anything. The man does not know the answer either. Why does modern life have to be so complicated? he wonders. He takes the gun from the closet, just to make clear what needs to be reckoned with if one crawls between his marital sheets and disregards his conjugal rights. His wife says, don't make a fuss, you're not going to do it, you don't have the guts, you're not man enough. You don't think I am? asks the man, you don't think I am? His friend takes him more seriously; the man knows the blotches on his friend's face are not from the summer heat alone. You don't think I am? yells the man, drawing the required determination from his friend's fear, you don't think I am, do you?

He grips the gun firmly and jams it under his friend's chin, then under his own and then back again. The beads of sweat oozing down his friend's face drop onto the gun, and the man does not like it at all, the situation is increasingly undignified. So he shifts the gun from his friend's chin to his own, to his friend's, faster and faster.

Well, tell me now, he yells at his wife, which one do you like better, which one should I eliminate? She tells him two more times that he's not man enough, that he's not what he's making himself out to be; each time she says it more quietly, then she starts begging him to put the gun away. That she'll call the cops otherwise.

Call them, go on, call the cops! says the man to her. Before you hang up we'll all be dead, and by the time the cops arrive, the whole house will have burned to the ground. He does not really mean this, he is just making threats, to create a fuss, to strike terror into their hearts and regain his self-confidence. What do people do when a thing like this happens to them? he wonders again. Understandably enough, nobody likes to talk about these things. Anyway, violence seems quite inappropriate, he's a gentle soul by nature, and, besides, he has seen that, despite this bit of nookie, his dinner is waiting for him in the kitchen, a golden-brown roast chicken keeping warm in the oven that reminds him that his woman is not so bad after all.

There's an earth-shattering bang as the bullet zips straight into the television set. He could swear the damn thing went off all by itself. Then everything is absolutely quiet again. Not even the wife screams, as might be expected, they all strain their ears to hear what happens next, who bangs on the door first. Nothing. The stony silence continues. As though nobody has heard anything.

Then the wife says softly: Well, and here I was, thinking we were finally going to meet the neighbors, and she bursts out laughing. The friend starts glancing around and the man guesses the reason for his uneasy fidgeting and tells him to get dressed, just in case the cops show up anyway, he can't meet the cops bare-assed, his wife and him can finish this hanky-panky some other time. The friend nods and starts pulling his pants on, then he asks the man if he has any idea how badly he is shaking. Perhaps I am, thinks the man, in this state I couldn't even hit myself if I wanted to, and besides, what do I want with a gun, this isn't my kind of thing. He carefully wraps it back in the T-shirt but then lays it on the table in front of him, to make it clear that he still calls the shots. His mouth is dry, he feels he could do with a beer, so he goes into the kitchen, to the fridge, but it's empty.

The man asks his wife where the hell all his booze has gone. The friend clears his throat and says, sorry, the day was so hot, what can you do, and besides, the man knows how hard it is for him to stop drinking once he starts. To make up for it he'd gladly invite the man for a drink to the bar across the street. The wife says she feels like having a beer too, so all three go there, have a round, and then another.

When they have knocked back quite a few and it is closing time and the waitress is about to throw them all out, the man says to his friend: Well, then, you take my wife with you and forgive me for scaring you, forgive my selfishness, I wish you happiness in your future life together, and if you have any money to spare you can buy me a new TV set and we'll call it quits. He realizes he sounds maudlin, but what the heck, he thinks, it's from the heart.

And his friend says no, you take her home, she's your wife, but first punch me. Yes, slug me, bust my nose and call me a son of a bitch. And if that's not enough, you know where I live, I expect my wife doesn't spend her mornings keeping her legs crossed either. And the wife says, even before the friend has had his full say and a proper man-to-man talk can develop: Don't fight over me, I'm not worth it. I suppose I should throw myself under a train or something, but life has its moments, I wouldn't want to miss them, I've missed too many already, you know what I mean? You . . . Well, you know.

That's true, says the man, actually there's still that chicken in the oven, keeping warm, why don't we go back to our place, I haven't eaten all day. Neither have I, the other two chime in, and they wheedle another round from the waitress, for the road, and then go home to eat chicken. So you're not going to beat me up? asks the friend as they pick clean the last bones, throwing them over their shoulders among the shards of glass, as the rough edges soften and the man finds the sight of the jagged jaws of the TV set increasingly familiar. The man motions no; is a thing like that worth mentioning at all? We're friends, aren't we?

Well, in that case I'd like to go home now, says the friend, it's very late, my wife will be worried sick, I'm a reliable guy, I always come home on time. You can't drive this drunk, the man urges him, you must stay the night, life's too precious, you shouldn't play with it. Okay, says the friend, alright, where do you want me to sleep? Don't get me wrong, I didn't mean anything by that, he corrects himself immediately.

The man is silent, looking at his wife. She is silent as well. How long has this thing been going on, actually? The wife keeps silent. You don't really want to know, do you? she says in the end. You know, life really is like a comic opera. What's the use of pretending? We all try so hard not to let it pass us by before we've had a chance to take notice. To somehow . . . Oh, you know: Somehow.

I don't understand, says the friend, what are you two talking about, do you always talk this way? I'm sorry, but I'm so sleepy I'll just crash here. And he slumps onto the living-room couch and starts snoring straight away.

Wife, says the man, your chicken keeps getting better, but—did I really deserve this? Just look at him, he didn't even take his shoes off. And I walk in on you with a guy like this! I'm sorry, says the wife, but he's your friend, you brought him into our house, you're the one who should've been more choosy. Unfortunately, I don't have many opportunities to meet men. My life, you know, has not exactly turned out the way I expected it would. And what am I supposed to do, spend it crying in secret? You know how it is, we all do the best we can. And, sorry, I'm tired too, it's been a long day. Why don't we go to bed? Don't forget you have to go to work tomorrow.

So they go to their bedroom, lie down and, like every night, hold hands. The man looks at the sheets and says: I hate these little flowers, we must get something else. The wife murmurs something indistinct, strokes his hand and immediately drops off, exhausted by her day, while the man stares at the ceiling for a long time, with the salty aftertaste of crisp chicken skin still on his palate, wondering whether he hadn't overpaid for the gun and whether he could find somewhere to trade it in for a good television set. Tomorrow, he decides, tomorrow he must ask his friend if he perhaps knows of some-body who'd be interested in such a swap. There must be people who have a use for a thing like that, these are troubled times, and getting more and more so. It's just as well the guy snoring on the couch with his shoes still on is his friend, he thinks as sleep overcomes him. If it had been somebody else, he could have really shot him, and then things might have gotten out of hand, and then there would have been no turning back. It's just as well.

The Surface

They park by the side of the road and the man looks at the car, concerned whether he has left it far enough onto the shoulder. Horrific images flick through his mind: some careless driver might graze it in passing! He glances at the car key in his hand, considers getting behind the wheel again and re-doing what's already done, but he can't bring himself to: If he did, the woman's lips would set into a thin, slightly quivering, disdainful line. You're incapable of getting anything right, the familiar sneer would be saying, you can't do anything right the first time, without having to correct it later.

The woman helps the child squirm out of his baby seat, then she takes the cloth-covered basket in which she's neatly, meticulously, thoughtfully packed lunch, exactly by the book for a Sunday family outing. The man pretends to be rapturously inhaling the fresh air smelling of ripe grasses, while he secretly contemplates the position of the car until the woman points out with unmasked irritation that the child has run on ahead and he'll have to follow.

The grass is tall, luxuriant, dark green almost, and striding through it the man has to admit it does not smell as fresh as he first thought; rather, it wafts a heavy, almost choking odor. As the little boy runs through the grass, the man can see him only from the waist up. He increases his pace, then realizes he won't catch up with the child this way. He shouts for him to stop, but the little boy only giggles and waves his arms in the air. The man wavers, glancing toward his car and his wife, who gestures for him to hurry up; so he breaks into a trot.

The boy suddenly, totteringly, stops dead in his tracks. The man rapidly approaches him, he's just a few paces away when he sees that the child is standing on the very edge of a canal that crosses the meadow, previously concealed by the grass. The little one teeters on the edge of the bank, turns his head to look at his father with huge, frightened eyes. Then he is pulled down by his own weight, down over the edge.

Springing forward with all his body, the man covers the few remaining paces in a single bound, he's on the edge, he throws himself into the emptiness, leaping after his child. Only when the murky, muddy water reeking of rot envelops him does he remember: He can't swim. But that's irrelevant now. Being the heavier of the two he sinks faster and deeper than the child, he feels around underwater for him, grips him around the waist and starts kicking as hard as he can. That's how swimming's done, he feels. That's what he tries, having no alternative.

His shoes slip off his feet and sink into the dark abyss beneath. The man feels that it's taking a very long time, too long, that they aren't moving at all, that they'll never come up to the surface. He also thinks in the time that has strangely compressed in his head that they can't have been under water for very long since the breath he took just before breaking the surface still seems sufficient, his lungs still feel pretty full of air.

Eventually he kicks his way up to the surface and pulls out his son. The child spurts a jet of putrid water and bursts into tears. The man feels the urge to hug the child close, tight, to just hold him and ignore everything else, absolutely everything in the whole wide world; then he feels the force of the water pulling him back down and he starts kicking again.

The woman is stretching her arms from the bank, and the man notices with astonishment that for the first time in all their years together he can read confusion in her face, uncertainty, admission that the world has surprised her, proven to her that there are times when she cannot lay down the law. He hands the child up to her; suddenly the little fellow is light as a feather, weightless, like when he was newborn, and just like then, when he held him in his arms for the first time, still wet with birth water, the child feels soft and willing to belong completely, all of him. The woman puts him down next to her and the little boy immediately hugs her thigh, worriedly watching his father, who is trying to find among the rocks supporting the bank a handhold with which to pull himself up.

Finally he succeeds: He drags himself up, his face so close to the dirt that he can see the tiny pores, the furrows made by ants, worms, and all kinds of minute creatures, so close that grit gets in his nostrils. He straightens up and attempts to smooth out and wipe clean his rumpled, soaking, filthy clothes. Then he realizes his gesture is ridiculous. Consciously he arrests it, and his arms float in the air in a strange, uncontrolled way. He looks at them flail, and thinks: Funny. Funny.

"How are you?" he asks the child. The child looks at him gravely. "Okay," he says. "Okay. I was afraid I'd keep going. Down there. In there." The child presses to him. The man can smell the mud and silt in the child's hair, and he signals to the woman to hand him the cloth covering the basket. Slowly and gently he dries his son's hair, and the boy looks at him unblinkingly while drops of water slide down his cheeks. Leaving a wet trail, muddy on the edges.

In the evening the man sits on the bench in the garden and smokes. The woman brings out a tray. Tea steams in the cups. "The little one's asleep," she says and touches her husband's cheek.

The man ponders her gesture. He thinks about the face he saw when his son and he had swum up to the surface. I won't let you get at me any more, he thinks. Now I know: We're equal. Equal. Neither of us knows how. You can't hide that from me anymore.

I'll quit my job, he thinks. It's pointless. The paperwork's all the same. Life's too short. And I have to say how I feel. Tell her too. It can't go on like this forever. Something's got to give. Also because of the little one. He could well have kept going down there. In there. And I with him. We could've both stayed under. But we didn't. We came out. And now we're staying here. On the surface. I'm not going to let you get to me any more, no way.

He flicks the half-smoked cigarette in the air and follows it with his eyes. The last one, he says to himself. The last one. The glowing dot hovers above him for a second, then takes a nose-dive and goes out. The man feels the open dome of the sky descending, embracing him, he senses the universe closing in, he smells the brittle trail of comets, the gravity of distant worlds brushes his cheek. Galaxies open up and beckon him in. The man knows: This is the beginning; this is just the beginning.

SLOVENIAN LITERATURE SERIES

DRAGO JANČAR
THE TREE WITH NO NAME
Translated by Michael Biggins

A diary recounting four decades' worth of sexual exploits, the memoir of a mental institution attendant, and a familiar-looking bicycle dredged out of a river–the discovery of these artifacts sends an archivist on an obsessive quest to discover their owners' identities and fates. Shifting between Slovenia's postcommunist present and its wartime occupation by the Axis powers, *The Tree with No Name* is Drago Jančar's masterpiece: a compelling and universally significant story of an individual confronting the constraints set on truth by his–and every–culture.

The Tree with No Name is published by Dalkey Archive Press in August, 2014.

Visit **www.dalkeyarchive.com**